WITCHSLAPPED IN WESTERHAM

Paranormal Investigation Bureau Book 4

DIONNE LISTER

Dionne Lister

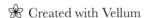 Created with Vellum

Coffee. You get me through every day. For that, I thank you.

CHAPTER 1

Beep. *Beep. Beep.*

I returned Olivia's grin as the gangly teen checkout boy scanned our chocolate choc-chip four-litre ice cream tub and put it in the bag. Our mini-grocery trip was almost done. The checkout guy's hand hovered over our bunch of bananas.

A man's voice came from behind us. "Hey, boy! Don't touch those."

Angus—his name tag proclaimed it so—froze. He looked up through his lank fringe at the scrawny old man whose grey trousers appeared to be trying to devour him like a giant python. The pants had managed to swallow his entire lower body up to his armpits. Impressive high pantsing.

The old guy shook his walking stick at the sign above him. "It says ten items or less."

Olivia and I looked at each other, and she shrugged. I turned back to the old man. "We only have nine items. I'm not the best at math, but last time I checked, nine was less than ten."

He reached across the conveyer belt and bashed my bananas with his cane. "There"—bash—"are"—bash—"five"—bash—"bananas"—bash. "That makes thirteen items, missy. You need to get your groceries and go to that line over there." He nodded to the register next to ours.

What in fresh hell was this? Now my bananas were probably only good for putting in a cake. I was going to have to go get another bunch. I folded my arms. "I'm pretty sure that the whole bunch is counted as one item. Isn't that right, Angus?" I turned to the teenager, eyebrows raised.

Angus stared at me, then at the old guy. "Um." He swallowed. "Yes," he squeaked, before leaning back, away from us. Pfft. Scaredy cat.

Angus edged his hand towards the bananas again, his eyes warily on our adversary. The old man shuffled forward and slammed his cane down. Poor Angus only just snatched his hand out of the way in time. Part of the cane squished the bananas some more, but the end hit the plastic edging on the conveyer belt. The loud *crack* attracted notice. Two cashiers down the line from us turned to watch. A few shoppers swivelled their heads to rubberneck as they wandered past. *Keep walking. Nothing to see here, people.*

If only that were true.

"You young people have no respect." The old man gritted his teeth as he spoke. "Now get out of this line. Ten items or less. Less!" He scowled, and his bushy white eyebrows came together like two hairy caterpillars kissing. I would have giggled at the visual if anger hadn't been radiating off him. His face glowed red. Yikes. His circulation was quite good for an old person.

I turned to Angus, to check if he'd put our bananas through. His gaze darted from me to python pants to the bananas, then to me again. "I think I'd like to get another bunch. These look ruined."

"Lily, look out!" Olivia's eyes were wide.

Thwack!

"Ouch!" Sharp pain lanced through my shoulder.

Thwack!

I turned and threw my arms up, and the cane that had hit my shoulder came down on my forearm. *Jesus, that hurt.* This was ridiculous. I sized up the crazed man, waiting for his next blow. The cane descended. I grabbed it and held it with both hands. "Are you nuts? You can't just hit people like that."

"Let go!" he screamed and yanked on the cane, but I wouldn't give it up. No way in hell.

Rage burned in his eyes. He tugged harder, and I needed all my strength to hold on, which kind of surprising considering he must have been seventy or more, and he was shorter and frailer than me.

Shoppers weren't wandering past anymore—they were stopping for the impromptu afternoon entertainment. Great. Would I be the bad guy if I hurt this man? I hadn't done anything, but now I feared for my safety.

"That'll be twenty-four pounds." Angus obviously thought if he pretended nothing was unusual, all the weirdness would disappear.

"Give me my cane!" the old guy bellowed. Crap.

I didn't want to take my attention away from my tug of war, so I called out to Olivia without turning. "Can you pay, please? I'll pay you back later. We'll just forget the bananas." Although that hurt almost as much as getting hit with the cane. The old moron would win. "Actually, go grab another bunch. I've been through hell for those damn bananas, and I'm not going home without them."

"Yeah. Not a problem. Ah, do you need any other help?"

"No. If you could just grab another bunch, that would be awesome."

"Coming right up."

I cocked my head to the side, assessing my opponent. *Come on, Lily, he must weigh about fifty kilos and have osteoporosis.* I adjusted my grip and braced myself. "Look, I don't want to hurt you, but I've had enough. I really want to go home and eat my ice cream, which is probably melting now." I was short of breath because he hadn't stopped trying to reclaim the cane. "Please just calm down and lower the cane."

"Never. I'll die before I let you get away with wrongly utilising the ten-items-or-less lane. There's a special place in the underworld for miscreants like you." His eyes shot death lasers at me. Well, they would have if it were possible. Oh, dear. It might be if he was a witch.

"How many times do we have to tell you? A bunch of

bananas is counted as one item. Don't blame me. I didn't make the rules. I'm just shopping by them." I engaged my second sight. Okay, he wasn't a witch, so I had to go easy. As much as he could bruise me, he wasn't about to strike me down with lightning or singe me with lasers.

He narrowed his eyes and leaned backwards, pulling as hard as he could.

"Security to the express register. Security to express." Well, it was about time someone made good use out of that loudspeaker. But I still needed to protect myself, or he could end up cracking my head open.

I knew I shouldn't because he was old, but I had warned him, not to mention that his behaviour was deplorable. You couldn't just go around assaulting people and expect no repercussions.

He leaned back further, determination etched into every wrinkle in his face. I pushed the cane and let go. He flew backwards and slammed into a huge, tattooed guy with a potbelly. The old man's saviour grunted as he caught him.

Then security turned up—two middle-aged blue-uniformed men, one so skinny he'd blow away in a storm, and the other overweight, sweat beading on his forehead. A woman in a white shirt and black skirt was with them, and she'd brought her scowl. "I'm Alicia Smith, manager on duty. She turned to the old guy. "Mr Anderson, good morning." Then she turned to me. "What exactly is going on?" Oh, great, they knew each other. I was the outsider in this situation, and things rarely went well for the outsider.

"My friend and I were going through this checkout with

nine items. That old man"—I pointed at him—"accused us of putting through more than ten items, and then he started hitting me with his cane. I could have him charged with assault." I narrowed my eyes and shot him my own death glare. Stupid old man.

She turned to the cashier. "Angus, did they have more than ten items?"

I blinked. That was the question she started with? Did nobody care that I'd just taken a beating? I would surely have bruises later.

"No, Miss Smith. They had nine." Angus turned and looked out the front doors, no doubt wishing he was somewhere else.

Mr Anderson had shuffled closer. He poked his stick towards Angus. "That's a lie, boy. Tell her about the bananas." He tipped his chin up, smugness radiating from every huge pore.

Angus swallowed. He looked at his superior and shook his head.

Alicia turned to Mr Anderson. "We count the same item as one item. One banana or ten, one tin of cat food or ten, they're considered one item."

Olivia had returned. She stood next to me and gently placed the new bunch of bananas on the conveyer belt. The old guy saw her. His mouth dropped open. "You can't be serious! This is not the England I grew up in. You're not going to let them get away with this, are you? This is a travesty!"

I didn't want to leave anything to chance. "Um, excuse

me, Miss Smith."

She turned to me.

"He also damaged our original bunch of bananas. Shouldn't he pay for them?" I tried not to smirk. I had the best interests of the supermarket in mind, but wouldn't that be awesome if he had to pay for those bananas he so hated.

Miss Smith nodded, but she wasn't smiling. I supposed she didn't want to treat any customer badly, but rules were rules. "Yes, he will." She turned back to Mr Anderson, whose eyes were wide. "You will apologise to..."

I couldn't help it, but I smiled. "Miss Bianchi."

"...to Miss Bianchi, and you will also pay for that bunch of bananas. If you ever assault another one of my customers, I will call the police. To be frank, Mr Anderson, I'm quite surprised at your behaviour." She shook her head.

The fire in his eyes dimmed. He probably realised this battle was over. He turned to me. He'd clenched his teeth, which didn't look all that apologetic to me. "I'm... I'm..."

"Mr Anderson." Alicia's voice held a warning tone.

He growled. "I'm... sorry. There, I said it. Happy now?" Talk about a constipated apology. That thing had not wanted to come out.

As much as the apology sucked, I just wanted to go home and eat my melted ice cream. "Apology accepted."

Alicia smiled. "There now. All done." She turned to me. "He's not usually like this, Miss Bianchi. I have no idea what's gotten him so riled up. I know it's within your rights to press charges, but if you could give him a break, I'd appreciate it. He really is a nice man, and he's too old to go through the trauma of being arrested."

I looked at Olivia. She shrugged. I sighed. I hated letting him get away with it, but he'd probably get off on an insanity plea, considering what had made him so angry in the first place. "Yeah, sure. But if he ever hits me again, I will."

"Thank you, Miss Bianchi." She turned to Angus. "Angus, no charge for those groceries today. It's the least we can do for Miss Bianchi."

Oh, well that was a nice outcome. "Thank you, Miss Smith. I appreciate it."

Angus bagged those trouble-making bananas. Olivia grabbed one of our bags, and I grabbed the other. As we walked out, heading for the public toilets, two women pushing shopping trollies stood facing each other, trolley noses touching.

The taller of the middle-aged women said, "Get out of my way, love. I was here first."

The other shook her head. "I was here first." She drew her trolley back and then slammed it into the other one.

"What the hell is going on today, Liv?" I considered helping the women sort it out, but I'd already attracted my share of trouble, and the crazy thing was that there was plenty of space for both women to go around each other. They were being stubborn for stubborn's sake.

"I was here first. *You* move!" There was another crash as the trollies came together, like a couple of rams headbutting for territory.

Olivia shook her head. "I have no idea, but I vote we get out of here before our ice cream becomes a milkshake."

"Awesome idea." We made our way back to the public toilets, the discordant trolley din following us. I *travelled* us both home to the delightful silence of Angelica's house.

I'd been practicing a lot lately, and now I was strong enough to travel another person. I'd also been learning new spells and working on my physical self-defence with James. After being warned by Drake to stop killing witches, I was determined not to kill anywitch else. And no, I wasn't a serial killer; I was just unlucky. It wasn't my fault witches kept trying to kill me.

We went straight from the reception room to the kitchen. I put the milk and cheese into the fridge. Then I opened the ice cream. "Hmm, it's not too bad." I poked it with a spoon. "It's soft but not runny. We'd better have some, just to make sure it's okay."

"You're right. We need to be sure." Olivia grinned.

I magicked us both bowls and another spoon out of the cupboard, and we served ourselves. Angelica had told me to use my magic as much as possible, to build up my witch strength. It took just as much effort to remember to magic stuff than it did to execute the spell. I was so used to doing things the normal way, that I'd often be in the middle of putting something away when I'd remember to magic it. This time, I was on the ball, and I ordered the ice cream into the freezer.

I sat opposite Olivia at the kitchen table and tasted the

chocolate choc-chip goodness. "Mmm, this is so good." I shut my eyes for a moment and savoured the taste.

"Mmm, you're right. It was worth getting smacked."

My eyes popped open, and I stared at Olivia. "Easy for you to say. You didn't get caned, literally." I put my spoon down and pulled the neck of my T-shirt down to expose my shoulder.

Olivia's eyes widened, and she bit her lip. "Oh, wow, that looks sore. That old guy was stronger than he looked."

I covered the purpling flesh. "Tell me about it. What makes a person lose it like that? And why do people have to be so stupid? He didn't even understand how the damn ten-items-or-less lane works." I comforted myself by shoving a spoonful of ice cream into my mouth.

Olivia shrugged. "I have no idea."

Brrring, brrring. Brrring, brrring. The antique telephone chime Olivia had as her mobile ringtone sounded. She reached into her bag and pulled out her phone. "Hello, Dad…. Yeah, not much. Just eating ice cream with Lily." As her dad spoke, her brow creased, and she frowned. "Oh, okay. I'll be right over…. Yes. Bye."

"What's wrong?" I had a funny twitchy sensation in the pit of my stomach. This wasn't going to be good news.

"Um, not sure, but Dad said Mum's taken a funny turn, and he's locked himself in their bedroom to get away from her."

"What? That doesn't make sense." Her mother was one of the most demure and gentle people I'd ever met. She didn't appear to have a crazy bone in her body, but as I'd learned multiple times recently, you never really knew a person. Maybe she'd gotten stuck into the booze or something. "Do you want me to go with you?"

"Ah, no. Dad would be mortified if he knew I told you anything. If I need backup later, I'll call you." She stood and put her phone back in her bag. She stared forlornly at the ice cream she was abandoning.

"I'll put it in the freezer. You can have it when you get back."

Her smile was half-hearted. She must be worried about her mum, although it could have been for the ice cream. "Thanks. I'll see you later." She turned and walked out.

I magicked her bowl into the freezer and finished eating. It was time to work on my spell to hide Millicent's baby bump so I could tell her about it when I had dinner at her place tonight. I'd almost gotten it, but I had a couple of words to tweak. If I got it wrong, she was going to look very strange, and I didn't want to do anything that would harm the baby. Glamours were tricky things. If you weren't careful, you could actually change someone's body instead of just making it look different.

I took myself to the spare bedroom where I'd set up a mannequin to practice on. How exciting: it would be me and an inanimate object for the rest of the afternoon. How had I ever thought my life was fulfilling before I was a witch? Ha ha. Somehow, I knew the joke was on me. It always was.

AFTER I'D WORKED ON MY SPELL FOR THE WHOLE afternoon, I took a shower and got ready to go see James, my brother, and Millicent. I knocked on Olivia's bedroom door at six thirty. She was coming with me. Tonight was the night we were going to explain my parents' situation and the diary to her. She was sitting her final exams to become a police officer in a week, and we really needed help with researching where my parents had been and who they'd been with.

She didn't answer, so I knocked again. "Olivia? Are you in there?" I opened the door a crack and peeked in. "Hello?"

Her bed was neatly made, and her desk was orderly—all her papers were in a manila folder, her pens were in a purple holder, and her laptop was closed. There was no Olivia. Hmm. She was never late, and we were supposed to be at my brother's at six forty-five.

I went to my room and grabbed my phone. "Siri, call Olivia."

"Calling Olivia."

"Thanks, Siri." I knew she didn't exist nor care about manners, but I couldn't help being polite. Siri was always so helpful.

Olivia picked up on the third ring. "Hey, Lily." Her voice sounded wary.

"Hi, Liv. I was just wondering where you were. We have to be at James's in ten minutes."

Her quick intake of breath sounded down the line. "Oh, my goodness! I'm so sorry. I won't be able to make it. My mum—ah, we've had some problems. I can't really talk to you about it now, but I won't be home till late. Please apologise to James and Millicent. I really am sorry, but my parents need me right now."

I knew she couldn't see me, but I pouted anyway. I was looking forward to dinner and finally opening up to Olivia about everything with my parents, but I'd get over it. "Ah, yeah, sure. Not a problem. Is there anything I can do to help? Is your mum okay?"

"She's alive and unhurt, but she's in hospital having tests. I'll let you know later, okay?"

"Of course. But call me if you need anything. Promise?"

"Yes, Mum."

I smiled. "Good. Now go do your daughterly duties, and don't worry about James and Millicent. They totally understand that family comes first."

She took a loud deep breath and blew it out. "Thanks, Lil. You're awesome. See you later."

I hated mystery. What had happened with her mum that she couldn't tell me, one of her best friends? And she was in hospital. That didn't sound good. I crossed my fingers that her mum was okay.

My stomach rumbled. I was totally looking forward to dinner. Millicent and James always cooked amazingly yummy food. I was about to ask Siri to call James when my phone rang, Millicent's name appearing on the screen. "Hey, Mill. I was just about to call you guys."

"Hi, Lily. I'm so sorry to do this to you and Olivia, but we're going to have to cancel tonight."

Huh? Wow, two cancellations in one night. I was going to get a complex. "Ah, that's fine. Olivia just rang me to cancel. Something happened with her mum, but I'm not sure what. Is everyone all right over there?"

"Yes, but we've both been called into work. The Kent police have been getting masses of call-outs. They can't keep up, and we're stepping in to help. Purely as non-witch government operatives, of course."

"But you can't go out and deal with criminals! What about the... you know what?" I didn't want to mention anything on the phone because you never knew who was listening.

"I'm going to be coordinating our agents from the office. Don't worry. I'll be safe. Anyway, I have to go. I'd already cooked, so I've sent some over to your place. There's enough for both you and Liv. It's in the fridge. Bye."

"Bye." I sighed. Well, so much for my fun night. At least I didn't have to cook. I didn't know enough magic to cook anything intricate yet, and we didn't have much food in the house, so I was glad Millicent had sent dinner over. I was sure Olivia would appreciate it when she got home too. Who knew if she'd had time to eat much today?

I went to the fridge. What surprise would await? I opened the door. There were six containers—three labelled "Lily" and three, "Olivia." I pulled my three out and took the lid off one. The cheesy aroma drifted into my nostrils. Oh my God. Eggplant lasagne. I grinned. James must have cooked. It was a recipe handed down in my dad's family. We'd had it in Italy when we visited our relatives, and Mum even learned how to make it. My mouth watered. I opened the next one, revealing salad with homemade Italian dressing, which was always olive oil, vinegar, and salt. The last container held three crepes filled with cooked strawberries and topped with a dusting of icing sugar. Ooh, the ice cream we'd bought this afternoon would totally go well with this.

I put the lasagne and salad on a plate and placed the crepes back in the fridge. There was a small snug at the front of the house, which we didn't use much. It had a TV, two-seater chocolate-colour leather couch, and one armchair, the fabric a pale blue-green. The ceiling was lower than in the sitting room, making it seem very snug indeed. If it were any lower, you could have called the room a claustrophobia. The English were used to these low ceilings, built when people had questionable nutrition, and everyone was shorter. But coming from Sydney, I was yet to adjust, and I didn't know if I ever would. High ceilings were much more to my liking.

I turned the TV on and sat on the couch, my dinner on my lap. Maybe there'd be something on the news about this supposed crime wave. I pointed the remote at the TV and flicked until I saw the local newsreader sitting at her desk. A red banner lined the bottom of the screen, white letters proclaiming: Breaking News.

"Over the last twenty-four hours, there has been an increase in violent crime in Kent. Today, the number of violent crimes escalated alarmingly. The Kent police have had to call in reinforcements from London and other government agencies to deal with this storm of violence and aggression. Our reporters were on the scene earlier today."

A video replaced her on the screen. Commentary came from a young male reporter who stood in front of a single-level brick building that had a huge sign at the front: "Miss Squirrel's Childcare Centre." A chain-link metal fence surrounded part of the building, which must have been the outdoor play area. Through the fence, children watched, their little fingers gripping the barrier, their tiny mouths hanging open. Some of them were crying. And honestly, I didn't blame them. What they were watching would upset anyone.

Three dads were punching each other, and two mums were screaming at each other, every second word being bleeped out. One of the mothers, an attractive brunette in designer sunglasses, white shorts, and a pink short-sleeved shirt, picked up her stroller—I assumed it was hers—and hit the other woman over the head with it. Ow! I scrunched my face. That had to have hurt. This was as bad as an episode of that American reality TV show—*Maury*. Oh, now one of the men was out cold on the ground, both the other guys standing over him, hands on hips.

The reporter looked incredulous as he alternated between watching the melee unfold behind him and looking at the camera in front of him. He was probably wary of being injured. "These adults have been fighting for the last twenty minutes, and it almost seems like it's going to be a fight to the death. The police were called a minute or two after it started, but they're stretched thin, and as yet, haven't attended. Nick Blair reporting for— Argh!" He hunched forward and dropped to the ground, out of camera range. Oh, dear.

The redhead who'd been hit with the pram had managed to wrestle it off her opponent, and she'd thrown it. The brunette had ducked out of the way, and it had slammed into the reporter. More like a tornado of violence than just a storm. Stuff was flying around.

"Nick. Nick, are you okay?" A male voice came from off-camera—probably the cameraman.

The scene blacked out, and then we were back with the presenter in the blessedly calm newsroom. Her eyes were wide. "Ah, scenes similar to that are being played out all over the county. No one knows why this is happening, but residents are being urged to stay home and away from others. If you have an emergency, be aware the police are taking longer to respond."

The screen behind her changed to a man dressed in long, white pants and white short-sleeved shirt. He had a red six-stitch cricket ball in his hand, and he was running in to bowl. The presenter continued. "In other news, Kent is in a winning position in their one-dayer against Somerset. Fast bowler—"

Click. I changed the channel, looking for more news. Another channel, another Breaking News banner. This time, a grey-haired news presenter sat behind a table in the studio. "In scenes reminiscent of *Lord of the Flies*, there was a massive brawl at an exclusive, highly respected school. Both male and female students at Sevenoaks School, twenty-two students in all, fought each other this morning. There were several injuries but nothing fatal. It is said to have started when students were asked to complete a group project. Our reporter on the scene, Anita Farmer, has more."

She stood outside the school with two teenage girls who were dressed in what I assumed was the Sevenoaks school uniform of a white shirt with blue-and-white-striped tie and dark skirt. The reporter gazed into the camera. "I'm outside Sevenoaks School with two students, Maria and Stephanie. These young ladies were inside the classroom when the fight started. They escaped without injury and didn't take part." She turned to the girls. "Can you tell me how it started?"

Maria nodded and pushed her maroon-framed glasses up her nose. "Well, it started because Marty Thompson took over our group. I mean, there are five in a group, and he does all the talking, plus he wouldn't listen to anyone else's ideas."

"Yeah," Stephanie cut in. "I wasn't in their group. I was in another one." Ah, yeah, Captain Obvious. I snorted. "And there's like, two girls and three boys, and the boys kept joking around, and us girls were doing all the work; like, that's just unfair. Anyway, Trudy, in my group, she got jack of it, and she pushed Michael over, like on his chair and everything."

"And in our group. Simon told Marty to shut up and give someone else a go, and he told him to... ah... can I swear on TV?"

"It's best if you don't." The reporter gave her an "I can't believe you just asked me that" smile.

"Well, he told him to eff word off, so Marty punched him in the stomach; then Peter, Simon's best friend, hit Marty over the head with his textbook. I just ran out, and then Steph met me in the hallway. It was madness. We could hear chairs hitting walls and people screaming."

The reporter nodded, a serious expression on her face. "Thank you, girls." She turned back to the camera. "So, there you have it. Back to you, Edward."

Click. This time I turned it off. Wow, it was all happening. But why? I was dying to find out, but I couldn't call Angelica and ask because she was helping deal with it. Had Olivia's mother been acting crazy like those other people? And was all this violence a coincidence, or was there something in the water? But there couldn't be. I'd drunk the water today, and I felt fine, and those two girls looked calm.

I'd managed to finish my dinner, but after watching the disaster unfolding around the place, I didn't feel like eating dessert. This was why I didn't normally watch the news. Life was depressing enough without hearing about how bad everyone else had it. Why couldn't only nice things happen? Why couldn't everyone just be happy and fair and be kind to each other? I sighed.

I grabbed my iPad, moved to the sitting room, and stretched out on a Chesterfield. Reading was a great escape. I'd read until Olivia got home. Then I could at least find out how her mum was and tell her what I'd seen on TV. Maybe they were related events? Hmm, and what about this morning, with the old guy? The store manager said he was normally very nice. Then those two women outside with the trollies. That wasn't usual behaviour for the people around here. I'd been here long enough to know.

I read for a while, until a key jiggling in the front door sounded. I shut my iPad case and stood. It must be Olivia. I met her in the hallway at the foot of the stairs. Her curly hair was up in a ponytail, but some of it had come loose, and she looked tired. She didn't smile.

"How's your mum?"

She looked at me, her dark eyes wide and glistening with tears. She took a deep breath. "She's still in hospital. They had to sedate her. This afternoon, she attacked my dad."

What the hell? "What with? Is he okay?"

She nodded. "Yeah, just a bit bruised. She punched, slapped, and kicked him."

I shook my head. That sounded just as crazy as all the news reports this afternoon. "Does he know why?"

"She was upset he left the toilet seat up." She wiped a tear away with the back of her hand. "They're going to keep her in the psyche ward overnight."

Crap. I bet he'd never forget to do that again. I didn't know how to help, so I suggested the next best thing to fixing anything. "Do you want some dinner, or maybe skip straight to dessert? Millicent sent our dinner over."

"Oh, she is so sweet. Did you apologise for me?"

"I did, but I didn't end up going anyway. She called just after I got off the phone to you. They had to cancel because work got busy."

"I thought you were home a bit early."

"So, food?"

"I'm not that hungry, but I could finish off that ice cream I started this afternoon."

I smiled and led the way to the kitchen. "Sit down. Let me get it for you."

She sat, and I grabbed the bowl out of the freezer and a spoon, then put them in front of her.

She blinked and studied her bowl. When she looked up at me, her brow was wrinkled and her eyes narrowed. That wasn't the reaction I'd been hoping for. "What's wrong?" I took a step back without even thinking about it. My subconscious clearly had my best interests at heart.

She wielded her spoon like a gavel as she spoke, striking the air after each word. "What. Is. This?"

I knew it was a trick question, but I answered anyway. "Ice cream?"

She shook her head. "This isn't all of it. There was more when I left. Did you eat some?" The glint of rage flickering in her eyes guaranteed that no matter how I answered, I was in trouble—admit to it and I was an ice-cream stealing cow; deny it, and I was a liar and an ice-cream stealing cow. My odds, as usual, sucked. And what was with her attitude?

Maybe if I didn't actually answer her in a direct way, we could avoid any unpleasantness. I shook my head and pointed to the freezer. I adopted the universal tone of voice of people trying to placate an angry child. I'd never had to use it before, but I'd heard it plenty of times in public, just prior to the meltdown that the kid apparently had to have. "I can get you some more. Would you like that?"

Her eyes weren't glowing red, were they? Ah, no, it was a trick of the light.

She banged the spoon on the table. I started, then stepped back again, towards the door. Olivia pushed her chair back, the bottom of it scraping across the floor and squealing. I knew things were bad when even a chair was scared. If I didn't heed the chair's warning screams, I was going to get beaten up for the second time today.

Olivia's fists were clenched. "No one steals my ice cream!"

My heart raced, and adrenaline zipped through my veins. There was definitely something weird going on. Olivia was the most passive person I knew. This was way out of character, and over ice cream that wasn't even missing.

I put my hands out in front of me, palms facing Olivia. "I didn't steal your ice cream. Honest. This isn't you, Liv. What's going on?"

There was no time to register what had happened before the slap of her palm across my cheek echoed in my ears and stung my skin. Jesus, that hurt. I put my palm on my cheek, incredulous. "Oh my God, Olivia. What the hell?"

She clenched her jaw and fist at the same time—the girl could multitask; I'd give her that. As she brought her arm up and threw her fist towards my face, I ducked to the side, turned, and ran. She wasn't giving out ice creams, and I didn't want seconds.

I raced up two flights of stairs, Olivia only a few steps behind. I beat her to my room and slammed the door. It had a lock, thank God, but I also sat against it, just to make sure. My breaths came quickly. I slowed them and tried to think.

Olivia banged on the door. "Let me in! Goddamn you!" *Bang, bang, bang, bang.* All I could think of was, thank God they had tight gun laws over here, or I'd be in big trouble.

The door vibrated with every fist fall. I'd left my phone downstairs, but even if I magicked it to me, I couldn't even call Angelica to come save me because she was busy. I'd have to think of a spell myself. Something that would stop her but not hurt her. Maybe I could put her to sleep? The only problem was that I didn't know any sleep spells, and it was so much easier to perform a spell on a person you were touching. Okay, that was two problems, but who could think straight when a maniac was trying to bash your door down?

I pushed my palms against my ears as I thought. Hmm. I'd need to make sure I said to only sleep for a few hours, in case I accidentally put her to sleep forever. This was no fairy tale, and there wasn't a handsome prince to save either of us if I got this wrong, not that we needed a man to save us. I was pretty sure we could save ourselves, provided no one got killed. And by no one, I meant me.

I tested a few different sentences until I came up with the one I assumed would work best. I blocked out the screams and thumping and imagined standing in a stream of the golden, flowing magic, then turned and placed my palms on the door. This was as close as I dared get to the raging maniac in the hall. "My friend, Olivia is banging on my bedroom door. Put her to sleep until tomorrow, and let her fall gently onto the floor." My palms tingled, and the door radiated warmth.

It was done.

I held my breath. The banging stopped, and a thud sounded from outside. I smiled. I was pretty sure it had worked, unless Olivia was trying to fool me. But I doubted that, as she didn't seem to be operating with any logic. It was pure anger and aggression without reason.

I called out, "Olivia, are you okay?" Silence. I stood and quietly unlocked my door. What would I do if I opened it and she was waiting to pounce? I could use a shield spell, which was for physical attacks, but it used a lot of energy, and I could end up falling asleep, which would be stupendously idiotic. And why did stupendous mean amazing when it sounded a bit like stupid? If I'd made up those words, I'd definitely have stupendous as meaning someone or something really stupid.

I put my ear to the door for a last-ditch check. The only thing I could hear was the blood swooshing past my eardrums. After a deep breath, I carefully opened the door a crack and peered through.

She was curled up on the floor in the foetal position, her hands, palms together, supporting her head. And was she snoring? Oh my God, she was. I laughed quietly—no sense in risking her waking up. It was likely my spell would last until tomorrow, but if my magic was weak, the spell would finish early. I'd tell Angelica before then and have her check that Olivia was going to stay asleep.

But what did we do when she woke up angry? I crossed

my fingers that the anger would be gone by then. I went to her room and grabbed her doona and put it over her. I bit my lip. I really should give her a pillow too, but I was too scared she'd wake up. Best to let the bear sleep.

I ducked downstairs, grabbed my phone, and called Angelica. It rang a few times before she answered, which was unlike her. She was usually Quick Draw McGraw when it came to her phone. "Hello, Lily." She sounded out of breath, and there was shouting in the background. "I'm a bit busy right now."

It sounded as if she was in the middle of an angry mob. "Is everything okay?"

Someone screamed, "Kill the copper scum!"

"Can you just get to the point? I'm in a *situation* at the moment."

"Sorry. Can you check Olivia when you get home? She went nuts and tried to beat me up, and I had to put her to sleep."

"Is she still breathing?" Her question was posed as calmly as if she were asking me if I'd like jam and cream with my scone. Nothing fazed her.

"Yes, of course. She's snoring on the hallway floor outside my bedroom."

"Okay, as long as she's alive. I have to go, dear. See you in a few hours." A scream came through the line just before she hung up. What the hell was going on out there? Was this the apocalypse?

I showered, got ready for bed, and locked myself in my room, just in case. I turned my laptop on. It was time to see what I could find out. Fear squirmed in my belly. *Please don't be chaos all over the world—well, more chaos than usual.* I mean, the world had been going to hell lately, but this was the underworld on steroids.

I googled "outbreak of violence USA." A few articles on mass shootings from the past couple of years showed up but nothing unusual. I shook my head at the fact that I thought that amount of horror wasn't unusual. I sighed. Now wasn't the time to get upset about all the things I couldn't change. I typed in the same phrase for Sydney. Nothing. Thank God my home city was okay. After a bit more research, it seemed as if the unusual amount of violence was concentrated in Westerham and a few other villages in Kent, with a small uptick in London. I'd love to see the police stats. They would probably point to Westerham being the centre with the problems radiating out in a diminishing circle. I'd bring it up with Angelica later.

I sent a quick email off to my two best friends back in Sydney, letting them know I was okay, just in case they'd seen anything on the news over there. Not that they were likely to. I shut my laptop and got under the covers. Hopefully when I woke up, this disaster would be over.

Unfortunately, hope was a slacker when it came to actually fixing anything. But right now, it was all I had.

CHAPTER 2

"**Y**ou stole my ice cream!"

I woke up, unsure if I'd been having a nightmare or if the shouting was real.

Thump, thump, thump. "I know you're in there, Lily. I'm going to kill you!" The door shook with each strike.

Okay, it was real. When was Olivia going to give up on wanting to hurt me? A massive bang landed on the door, accompanied by a crack. Looked as if my door wasn't going to survive her attack. There was only one thing to do.

I jumped out of bed and hurried to the door. Once my palms were against the timber, I repeated my spell from last night but with a minor change. "My friend, Olivia is banging on my bedroom door. Put her to sleep until this evening, and let her fall gently onto the floor."

Thud. Silence. I listened for a moment, then carefully unlocked and opened the door a crack, ready to slam it again if need be. I smiled. Sleeping Beauty was snoring again. I opened the door all the way. There was a depression at about thigh height and a hairline crack in the wood. She must have kicked it—she hadn't removed the sneakers she'd been wearing yesterday.

How long would this episode last? What if she never calmed down? I swallowed as nausea bubbled up from my stomach into my chest. What if none of the angry people ever turned normal again? Was it a virus, kind of like when people became zombies? Okay, zombies didn't really exist... or did they? I'd never thought witches existed till I found out I was one.

Crap.

I shut and locked my door again, just in case, and checked the time. Five thirty. Argh, I hated getting up early unless I had something fun to do, and protecting myself from a crazy person was not my idea of fun. I threw on a T-shirt and shorts and grabbed a cardigan. It might be summer, but you never knew when the UK forgot what season it was supposed to be, unless it was winter—the UK was good at winter. I grabbed my knapsack with my camera, phone, and wallet. The hallway was still quiet, so I opened the door and stepped over Olivia. "Sorry," I whispered.

All of the noise this morning should have woken Angelica, provided she was even home. I knocked on her bedroom door. Nothing. I opened it to an empty room with an immaculate bed. Things were not going well if she hadn't come home. It was obvious the PIB needed all the help it could get.

I called Angelica. She answered on the second ring. "Good morning, Lily. You're up early. How's Olivia?" At least there was no war going on in the background this time.

"She woke me by banging on my door and threatening to kill me. I guess that answers your question. I'm coming into the PIB to help. I'm sure you could use an extra pair of hands." I didn't particularly like the place. If being arrested and spending time in their gross toilet-scented cells weren't bad enough, the boss, Drake Pembleton, and Agent Dana were enough to turn me off for life, but James, Millicent, and Angelica needed me. Westerham needed me.

"Thank you, Lily. We could definitely use your help. I'll see you here in a minute. Your usual rate of pay applies."

"Oh, but I'm not doing anything special."

"Doesn't matter. Everyone's on extra pay because they're working double shifts, and like I said: we need you."

Well, if she wanted to pay me lots of money, who was I to argue? "Okay, thanks. Bye." I hung up and made my door to the PIB reception room.

I looked through the small glass square on the reception-room door. A familiar middle-aged face stared back at me, one I hadn't seen for a while. The door opened. "Hello, Gus! Long time no see." I smiled as I stepped into the hallway.

He smiled and shut the door. "Welcome back, Miss Lily. I see you've learnt a thing or two since I saw you last."

"That I have. How's your wife doing?" Last time I'd seen him, his wife had just had her gallbladder removed.

"She's doing rather well. She can't eat rich foods

anymore, so black pudding Sundays have gone out the window, but what can you do?" He shrugged.

I tried to keep my face from scrunching. Ew, black pudding, which was essentially coagulated blood. If someone handed me some, it would definitely be out the window. She'd just done them both a favour, and he didn't even realise.

Gus started walking down the corridor. "I'll be taking you to Ma'am. She's in the control centre."

"Sounds good. Thanks, Gus."

"My pleasure, Miss Lily."

We took a few turns and came upon a lift I hadn't seen before. It was at the opposite end of the complex to the other lifts, although that was a guess on my part, taking into account where we'd walked. These corridors had no windows, so I could've been turned around and not realised. Gus waved his security tag across a sensor, and within half a minute, the lift arrived.

The floor numbers in the lift were 2, 1, G, B, B1, B2, and B3. Gee, this place had more basement floors than above-ground ones. The lift stopped at B3. We stepped out, and Gus turned left. We walked to the end of the hallway, which ended at a blank white wall. Okay, that was weird. Ooh, maybe there was a secret door.

We stood there, waiting. And waiting. Hmm, white floors, check. White walls, check. White ceiling, check. *La de da da.* I caved. I didn't do well with standing quietly in confined areas with people I hardly knew. "So, Gus, no more black pudding, huh."

He nodded, his face sad. "Aye, miss, no more black pudding."

"Has your dog been vomiting lately?" I hated small talk, but being in this enclosed space with no sound was really getting to me.

"Actually, he vomited yesterday, but he did it on the tiles in the kitchen. Lucky for me, he ate it again. I just had to give the floor a quick mop."

I gagged and covered it by coughing. "That's great news." Why had I instigated this conversation? Oh, that's right: I was feeling uncomfortable. How had I managed to make it worse?

Then, a rectangular section of wall, the size of a door, moved backwards a couple of inches, then silently slid across, revealing Ma'am. She was in her PIB gear: white shirt, black pencil skirt, and jacket; however, her tie was missing. Her hair was in its usual immaculate bun, but there were dark circles under her eyes. "Hello, Lily. Welcome to the control room. Thanks for bringing her down here, Gus."

"My pleasure, Ma'am." He gave a respectful nod, then turned to me. "It was lovely seeing you again, miss."

"Likewise, Gus. See you later."

As Gus strolled back down the way we'd come, Ma'am led me into the room, and the door silently closed.

The room was quite large, probably four times the size of the conference room. Grey carpet covered the floor, and the walls were standard PIB white. Several manned workstations lined the walls, each one with a desktop computer and phone. A conference table surrounded by eight chairs took up the middle of the room, and the far wall was covered with TV screens, each one showing a different scene. Some were outside, in downtown Westerham—I recognised Costas in one of the pictures—a couple of screens showed what looked like interrogation rooms or cells, and the others showed the streets of other villages, some from fixed cameras, and a couple from what must be body cams. Unfortunately, most of them showed people hurting other people or damaging property. You would have thought that at six in the morning, not much would be happening, but you'd be wrong.

The low hum of voices buzzed through the room along with a sense of energy borne of action and purpose. People hurried from one end of the room to the other, handing each other documents, asking questions, or pointing to one of the screens. Phones were answered and hung up and answered again. I didn't spy any familiar faces. "So, Ma'am, what do you need me to do?"

"It would be wonderful if you could give me some of your magic and replenish my energy, but since that's impossible, I'll get you to answer the phones. At the moment, we're dealing with whatever overflow the police send us, which is a damn lot, to be honest." She must be feeling the stress since she never let loose like that. And yes, that was Ma'am letting loose. She lowered her voice. "If we don't get things under control soon, we'll have to call the army in. I've never seen a situation like this before. It's unheard of."

She led me to the only vacant desk with a computer and phone. "The calls we're getting are straight from outside, so you'll be talking to the public. Make sure to answer the phone, Kent Emergency Services. What is your emergency?"

"Okay, I can do that."

"Once you've answered the phone, remain calm, no matter what they tell you. Ask for their full name, their location, and what their emergency is. Each time you answer the phone, a page will come up on the computer. I want you to type in all the details there, and make sure to ask how to spell all names—we don't want to go to the wrong house, for instance. Once the call has ended, click on the Process button, and that will send it through to the next stage. You'll also have to decide which type of emergency service they need and tick these boxes." She pointed to the screen, which had either a Police, Ambulance, or Fire next to each box.

My brain raced. What if I got something wrong and didn't get help to the person in time? I licked my bottom lip. This was a lot of responsibility.

"You can do it, Lily. It's easy. If I didn't think you were capable, I wouldn't have asked you to help. Besides even someone making a mistake is better than no one, and we're quickly running out of agents to replace the exhausted ones."

"I'm nervous, but I'll be fine. You can count on me." I smiled.

"Good. Now, quickly, before you start, what happened with Olivia?"

I told her about this morning, and she frowned.

"I was hoping it would have worn off sooner." She blew

out a heavy breath, closed her eyes, and pinched the bridge of her nose before composing herself. "We're either dealing with a virus or magic that only affects non-witches. But that's about as much as we know. We're holding some of those arrested because Kent police have run out of cells, and they can't put people together, or they attack each other." She shook her head. "We've been doing what you did and putting sleep spells on everyone so we can have more than one in a cell. It's getting tricky because we're running out of space too."

"So you don't know how long this thing lasts or where it came from?"

"No. We're running various tests on the detainees here, so hopefully we'll have an answer soon. Okay, Lily, time to get to work. If you need anything—food, drink—just press this button on your phone"—she pointed to a blue button at the bottom of the landline phone—"and Felix will come on the line and take your order."

"Who's Felix?"

"He runs the cafeteria upstairs. He'll send someone down with whatever you want."

"Okay, thanks."

A short, wiry man in a PIB suit and tie appeared at Ma'am's shoulder. His front teeth stuck out, and when he gave Ma'am a jerky nod, he looked like a rat. I expected him to cup his hands and use them to clean his ears and face at any moment. "Ma'am, can I see you for a moment, please?"

She turned to him. "Of course, Agent Wilson." They

walked away, and I sat and answered my first call. My mind blanked. Crap. Oh, that's right. "Good morning, Kent Emergency Services. You're speaking with Lily. Can you state your name and your emergency?"

"Myra Wilson. My husband got a knife and slashed my favourite curtains. Now he's threatening to cut up our quilt covers." She sniffed as if she'd been crying. "I don't know what to do. Please help. He's never liked those curtains, and he says the floral print on the bed is too girly, but I never thought he hated them enough to kill them."

Kill them? Whilst murdering curtains wasn't illegal, this was a tough one. On one hand, he had a knife and wasn't afraid to use it, but on the other, he was only attacking inanimate objects, except what if he got angry enough to use it on her? "Can you spell your name please and give me your address. We'll have someone there as soon as possible." Whether this would be deemed an emergency or not was someone else's decision, thank goodness.

She gave me all the details, which I typed into the computer. I pressed Process, then answered my next call. Before I knew it, four hours had passed. I tilted my head to one side, then the other to stretch out the kinks. And was that a grumble coming from my stomach region? I did believe it was.

I held the receiver to my ear and pushed the blue button. Felix came on the line, and I ordered a cappuccino, a toasted cheese and tomato sandwich, and a chocolate-filled croissant. That should keep me going until the afternoon.

"Can I have everyone's attention please?" Ma'am stood in front of the wall with the TV screens. Grrr. My least favourite person was standing next to her: Dana Piranha. "I'm going home to have a couple of hours' sleep. While I'm gone, Agent Lam will be in charge."

Oh, great, just what I wanted, to be lorded over by that b—

"We've also had news that the people the police locked up yesterday morning, when this whole thing started, have calmed down. They remember what happened but claim it felt like a dream. Most were shocked to discover they'd been violent in real life. We'll have a meeting when I come back in later this afternoon. Great work, everyone. Now back to it." Angelica said something to Dana, walked towards the doorway, and left.

Piranha threw me a narrowed-eye gaze. Was that supposed to intimidate me? I smiled and waggled my fingers in a sarcastic wave. She curled her lip into a sneer. Good, I annoyed her. While that had been my goal, I couldn't totally shut out the voice that whispered, "Don't poke the piranha." Fine. I took heed of that inner voice and turned back to my computer.

Just as I was about to answer a call, a tray popped onto my table with my food order. Oh my God, yum! The coffee was in a large mug. I brought it to my nose and sniffed. My eyes practically rolled into the back of my head. I so needed this caffeine fix. I took a sip. Mmm, so good.

"What are you doing?" Piranha stood next to my desk, her arms folded, fin… ah, foot, tapping on the floor.

"Having lunch. I haven't eaten at all today. Ma'am said I could order food and drink when I needed to."

She glared at me and pressed her lips together. She was probably trying to figure out how to get me into trouble, and I bet she would've taken my food away if she could have. I'd dropped Ma'am's name into the conversation to let her know I would totally be telling her boss about anything horrible she did to me while there were no witnesses.

"Well, hurry up. You're not paid to eat lunch." She turned with an exaggerated sweep of her head, her glossy straight hair flinging around like in a shampoo ad. All she needed was a galloping horse, and the scene would be complete. Drama queen.

After finishing my food, I got back on the phone. The calls had slowed somewhat, but that was probably because three-quarters of Westerham's population was already incarcerated. Would everyone have a criminal record after this, or would the police agree it had been an anomaly and let them off with a warning?

I looked at the time. Four o'clock. Had Olivia woken yet? What if she was still angry? What if she never returned to her normal happy self? My leg bounced up and down under the table, and I crossed my fingers. *Please be okay, Liv.* I looked at my phone sitting on the desk and resisted the urge to call Angelica to see how things were going at home. She needed sleep. I'd just have to be patient. Gah. I bit a fingernail.

"Ugh, disgusting habit."

I looked up at Piranha whose expression said, "I just ate someone else's snot, and I did not like it."

I shrugged. It wasn't the best habit in the world, but it was far better than eating snot.

"I have a job for you, *petal*." She snorted. Ha ha, I got it. Lily was a flower, and she was also using petal as a term of anti-endearment, or would that be en-hatement? Whatever. I was not going to react.

"Yes, Agent Laaaam. What can I do for you?" I smiled innocently, as if I hadn't just bleated her name. Okay, so I wasn't meeting my goals today. What could you do? I was happy I'd found a new name for her though, one that made her seem less menacing. Piranha was so last week.

Her nostrils flared, but then she smiled almost as sweetly as I had. "I need you to collect a large envelope from the front desk and bring it back to me."

"Why don't you just magic it here?"

She rolled her eyes. "This room is warded against magic use for security purposes. Food can be magicked down, but that's the only allowance in the protective wards. If you had half a brain, you'd know that. Anyway, don't worry. Collecting the envelope is a job even a child could do, so you should be able to manage. It will have my name on it: *Agent Dana Lam.*" Condescending much?

"Is that one 'a' in Laaaam or three?" I gave her a closed-mouth smile.

She narrowed her eyes and bent to get in my face. Her clenched jaw was only inches from my ear. "You'd better watch yourself around here, *petal*. Like I told you before: I'll find out your little secret, and then I'm going to use it against you. The PIB is no place for losers with no talent. And guess who agrees with me?"

I kept my face impassive because she was surely going to bring up Will, and I wasn't going to give her any satisfaction by reacting, for real this time.

"That's right, child: Will. He wants you out of here just as much as I do. I've seen the way you look at him. I feel embarrassed for you, and so does he. You're pathetic. Now, go and get my envelope like a good little girl, and maybe I'll give you a lollipop when you return. Tell anyone I threatened you, and I'll deny it. I'm very good at *persuasion*—it's one of my talents. And if that's not enough to discourage you..." She smiled and half closed her eyes, as if she was going to tell me a delightful secret. When she spoke, her breath feathered my ear, and I shuddered. "I will hurt those you love in ways you can't imagine. Again, warning anyone won't get you anywhere. I'm respected around here, and no one will believe your word against mine once I explain my side of the story." She stood straight and looked down at me, her gaze hard, menace oozing from her perfectly made-up pores. Her fake eyelashes probably doubled as poison-tipped mini throwing weapons—rip them off, fling, and Bob's your uncle.

Wow, she really wanted to get rid of me. But why? Did she see me as some kind of threat to her job or for Will's affection? I knew I should feel scared, and I did a tiny bit, but I'd never let anyone intimidate me before, and I wasn't about to start. It was time to call her bluff.

I stood and met her stare.

"Hmm, someone got up on the wrong side of the field this morning. But don't worry, I'll be happy to get your envelope. I'll be baaack soon." I walked out and left Agent Laaam glaring at the back of my head. It felt good to stand up for myself. Bullies sucked, and they loved an easy target. The best way to deal with them was to give as good as you got.

It wasn't till I reached the lift that I realised I may have made a huge miscalculation. Agent Lam wasn't just a bully: she was a sociopathic narcissist who could use magic.

Oops.

When would I ever learn?

CHAPTER 3

After returning with Dana's envelope, I stayed out of her way for the rest of the afternoon. Antagonising her was just asking for trouble, and I couldn't help it. Best to avoid the opportunity altogether. I was not to be trusted.

At 6:00 p.m., Ma'am returned and took over. She had some good news too—Olivia was back to her normal, sweet self. "It's safe for you to return home, Lily. You've worked a long day here, and we may need you tomorrow. We still have no idea how this all came about, and once everyone's been processed and released, it may happen again."

My eyes widened. "Again? Can the police handle that? I mean, according to the news, and a couple of the calls I took today, there were murders as well as assaults and general bad behaviour. What if this isn't the end of it? And if magic is somehow to blame, will those people be held accountable? Because I know Liv would never have acted that way if she were in her right mind."

"We have yet to work out the details. Let's figure out where this is coming from before we worry about the rest. From all the tests we've done, we haven't found any magic, and no viruses so far. It's rather puzzling. We're having to interview everyone. Once the police do their interviews, we're going to collate the information and see what similarities emerge." Ma'am's phone rang.

"I guess I'll let you get back to it. Good luck."

"Thanks." She put the phone to her ear. "Hello. Agent DuPree speaking."

I waved and made my way into the corridor before conjuring my doorway to Angelica's. Even though Ma'am had given me the all-clear, I was still worried. Maybe the violent people were only violent with the first person they came across who annoyed them? Seeing me might set her off again for all I knew.

I unlocked the reception-room door and opened it just enough to look out. Maybe I should call out to her, and if she screamed she wanted to kill me, I could just shut and lock the door again. I swallowed, licked my lips, and called out, "Olivia. I'm back. Hello. Olivia?"

"Lily? Where are you?" Footsteps hurriedly clomped down the stairs, but her voice sounded normal enough.

I stepped out, my heart thumping. "I just got home."

She reached the bottom of the stairs and met me in the

hallway. My shoulders relaxed, and I sighed out a relieved breath. "How are you feeling?"

She bit her lip. "I'm so sorry, Lil. Angelica told me what I did. I mean, I vaguely remember what happened, but it didn't feel real. I can't believe I tried to kill you, and I slapped you. I'm so, so sorry." She shook her head, and her eyes filled with tears. "Can you forgive me? I'll understand if you don't want to hang around with me for a while." Her brow wrinkled as she watched for my reaction.

I smiled and stepped towards her. "I won't lie—you scared the absolute crap out of me, but I knew it wasn't you. I will admit I'm worried it'll happen again. Do you have any idea what set you off?"

"I would've said the stress of seeing my mother flip out, but Angelica explained what's been going on. We went through everything I did that day, but nothing stood out as unusual."

"Maybe your mum had finally had enough?" I shrugged.

She vigorously shook her head. "No. My mother vents to me if she gets angry with Dad. She never even spanked me when I was a kid. She hates violence."

"Well, that is weird then. Do you want to sit down?"

"Yeah, sure."

We shuffled to the sitting room and each sat in an armchair by the fireplace. The worry lines in Olivia's forehead hadn't budged.

"Have you heard anything about how your mum's doing?"

"Dad called a couple of hours ago. Mum's fine now and back home. She's as mortified as I am about what she did. I really am so sorry. You're the last person I'd want to attack." She gave me a wan smile, then stared into the empty fireplace.

"Well, let's figure out what happened so we can make sure it doesn't happen again." I pictured my notebook and felt-tipped pen that were currently sitting on my closed laptop in my bedroom. Then I dipped into the golden river of power and imagined them in my lap. They arrived. Magic was so cool. I grinned and took the cap off the pen. I opened my notebook. "I know you've already gone through this with Angelica, but maybe we'll figure something out she couldn't. Do you mind telling me everything that happened when you left here? And don't leave anything out. The smallest thing might have significance."

"Well, I went straight to my parents'. Nothing happened on the way. By the time I got there, Dad had managed to escape the bedroom. He let me in, and together we…" She blew out a heavy breath. "She wouldn't listen to reason, and she was still trying to attack Dad, so we forced her into the car. It was horrible. She was screaming the whole time and trying to hurt Dad. I almost copped a fist to the face a couple of times. I still can't believe that was my mum."

I placed my hand on her arm. "It wasn't really her, just like it wasn't really you. I truly believe that. Something sinister is going on, Liv. It's pretty obvious. I mean, for half of Westerham to go psycho on the same day?"

She nodded and told me the rest of the story. They'd taken her straight to hospital to have her sedated and had to wait since there were so many other people in the same situation or injured. After three hours, she was admitted and sedated. Once sure she was okay, they'd gone to the hospital cafeteria for tea and pudding.

"Did the food or tea taste weird? Did you feel any different after having it?"

"No. And I spoke to Dad this afternoon. He was fine."

"And you came straight home afterwards?"

She nodded. Wow, that wasn't much to go on. If it were a virus, how come her dad didn't get it? And if it had been the food, he would have gotten it too, unless it was someone working at the cafeteria, and they only put something in every other meal? But then, before this started, I doubted half of Westerham had just been to the hospital and eaten there. It's not like it was *the* place to eat. I snorted. Things would have to be pretty bad on the restaurant scene for people to be seeking to dine at a hospital cafeteria.

"So, what do you think?" Olivia looked at me and bit her bottom lip. "Will it happen again? What if it's not safe for you to be around me?" Her brows drew together.

I shut my notebook. "I don't know. I'm sure we'll have more answers when Angelica collects all the data from everyone who was arrested. Maybe we should go talk to your parents, see what your mum did yesterday."

She shook her head vigorously. "No way. I'm sorry, Lily, but there's no way my parents would want anyone to know what happened yesterday. I told them that I told you that Mum came down with a twenty-four-hour vomiting thing, and we had to take her to hospital. They're very private people, and Mum would be mortified if anyone we knew found out what happened."

"Do you think you could ask her, see what you can find out? You don't have to tell her why you're asking. Tell her what happened with us last night and that you want to get to the bottom of it so it doesn't happen again." I laid my hand on her arm again because her hesitation in answering wasn't a good sign. "Please, Liv. If it wasn't important, I wouldn't ask. Surely you don't want this continuing?"

She snatched her arm from under my hand and hugged herself. "Of course not! It's just... what if we find out it's permanent? What then?" Her pupils were huge, almost engulfing all the brown of her irises. I took a deep breath to calm the voice in my head that agreed with her. It wasn't time to consider the worst-case scenario just yet.

"I don't know, Liv. But let's not worry about that yet. My gut tells me it's not permanent. Surely you'd still be enraged if it was?"

"Maybe. Or maybe I'm like a werewolf now, and once a month, I'll turn into a stark-raving-mad killer?" One corner of her mouth quirked up. "You know that's not such a crazy idea, considering witches exist, right?"

"I know. I've had to keep a very open mind lately. But I'm pretty sure this is an anomaly. And if it is a once-a-month thing, we'll just chain you to your bed when it happens." I grinned.

Olivia laughed. "Okay, I'll talk to Mum, but I don't know how it'll go. She may not want to talk about it. I'll do my best."

"And don't go anywhere else. It's still dangerous out there. Some of the phone calls I got today were… horrifying. Our little part of the world has gone mad. Maybe I should come with you and just sit in the car?"

"No, I'll be fine. I'll call you if anything happens. And I won't eat anything while I'm out, just in case."

"Okay. But be careful."

We stood and hugged. After she left, I turned on the TV. It was more of the same as yesterday, although the violence had slowed because so many people had been arrested, but it was still over the top. I was just about to turn the TV off when I came across a breaking news bulletin. A young male reporter wearing a blue shirt stood outside Tonbridge Police Station. "Kent residents are urged to stay in their homes tonight as the recent scourge of violence spreads to the police department itself. One policeman assaulted another, hitting the victim's leg with his baton this afternoon after an argument about who had to write an arrest report. We've spoken to some of the recently released offenders who claim there have been physical fights inside the Tonbridge Police Station between other officers. Four officers have been arrested by their colleagues, pending further investigation."

"Oh, crap." What would happen if more police were affected? Who was going to arrest everyone and get things under some semblance of control? Would they call the army in now? The PIB couldn't be expected to handle everything without magic, which was our agreement with the government—witches weren't to use magic on non-witches unless you had their permission, or it was in a non-harmful way to aid an investigation. Since most non-witches didn't know about us, using magic to restrain thousands of people was out of the question.

I wanted to call Angelica and see what was going on, but she didn't need my interruption, and what could I do anyway? I was just one little witch, one with limited experience at magic or law enforcement. Argh. I turned the TV off and looked out the window at the front garden. What was happening out there? Was Olivia okay? Sitting here doing nothing was going to make me crazy, but I couldn't go anywhere without an escort, and all the agents were occupied with far more important things.

I wandered aimlessly around the ground floor a couple of times, going into every room, doing a lap, then coming out again. At the end of two laps, I found myself in the kitchen staring at the freezer. Well, it was apparent what I wanted, and since there was nothing else to do, I may as well.

I sat at the table and magicked myself a spoon and a bowl of the ice cream that had caused so much trouble. When life went to hell, at least food still tasted good.

AFTER THE STRESSES OF THE DAY AND GETTING UP SO EARLY,

I was shattered and in bed by ten thirty. Olivia hadn't gotten home yet. I texted her to make sure she was okay. Then I went to sleep. We'd agreed to go through her mum's information in the morning. Besides, my brain was much smarter when it wasn't half-asleep.

I got up at 8:00 a.m. to find a note on the floor next to the door. It was from Olivia. She'd written down everything her mum had told her. I dressed and took the note with me downstairs. I'd need coffee before I went through it. Angelica was already sitting at the kitchen table with a cup of tea, dressed in her PIB suit.

"Good morning, Lily. Did you sleep well?"

"Yes, thanks. What time did you get in?"

"Just after three. We had quite the evening. How was Olivia when you got home?"

"Back to her normal self, from what I could tell." I smiled. "I saw that thing on the news, about the police being affected."

"It was bound to happen, since whatever this is affects non-witches. Drake, James, Dana, and I had a meeting with Chief Constable Alan Miller of the Kent police and Major Ronald Cromwell last night. We've drawn up a plan that will begin this afternoon. I've arranged a briefing for this morning. I'd like it if you came."

"But I'm not an agent. Will Dana be there?" I wasn't scared of her, exactly, but I didn't feel like dealing with her snide looks and derogatory comments today.

"Yes, she will, Lily. She's an integral part of our team.

You really need to get along with her. I'm not sure what your problem is." She raised her brows.

My mouth dropped open. Had Dana already been in Angelica's ear, turning her against me? That evil witch. Maybe it was better if I was there, so I could make sure she didn't bad-mouth me to everyone else. "Okay. I'll go. What time?"

"In thirty minutes." Angelica finished her tea and stood. "I'm off now. See you in the conference room shortly." She popped her cup away, and then she disappeared.

I magicked the coffee machine into making me a cappuccino, and when it was done, it floated to the table and set itself down in front of me. I grinned. It was like having a servant, but I didn't have to feel guilty for asking someone else to do it for me. I called my notebook and pen from upstairs. They appeared on the table. I opened the notebook and read through my scribblings from last night. Then I read the note Olivia had slipped under my door. Her mother had gone out that morning to a local teahouse to meet a friend. She'd eaten scones and had tea. After that, she went to a doctor's appointment, then home. The aggression started about an hour later. Unfortunately, there was nothing about the friend she'd met. Had that woman come down with violence too? That sounded funny, but that's what made sense to me. It was as if they'd caught it.

So far, the only common thing Olivia and her mother had done was eat something and drink tea, but if her mum had caught it at the doctor's, she could have passed it onto Olivia. But her dad hadn't gotten it, and he'd done everything Olivia had. I sighed. If only I could talk to Olivia's mother's friend. Maybe something would make sense.

I finished my coffee and frowned. I hadn't had a double-chocolate muffin in days. I missed my visits to Costa. Maybe I could sneak up there later without telling anyone. I hadn't seen any new goons since I'd killed the last one, and I knew more magic now. No one would miss me anyway since everyone was caught up in the disaster. I'd pop into the local public toilet, hurry into Costa, then pop home again. Easy peasy.

Decision made, I stood. I left my notebook on the table and magicked my phone into my back shorts pocket. It was time to go and face Agent Laaam. I snorted. I probably should take her threats more seriously, but cowering in fear was not my way, plus I was stubborn, and I hated the thought that she took pleasure from intimidating me. If it was going to make her happy, I was not going to do it.

I stepped through my doorway into the PIB reception room. Gus was there to open the door for me again. "Hey, Gus. Long time no see." I smiled.

"Good morning, Miss Bianchi. You're here almost as much as I am these days. When are you going to make it official?"

We walked side by side to the conference room. "Probably never. I don't want to be an agent. Ma'am just wanted me to sit in, although I'm not sure why, exactly."

"Ma'am has a reason for everything she does. I would bet that you're more help than you realise." He smiled.

I wasn't comfortable with this conversation, so I changed

the subject, and we chatted about nothing much until we reached our destination. As Gus knocked on the door, then opened it, my mouth went dry. I wasn't sure if it was because I was going to see stupid Agent Laaam, or if it was because I hated making a grand entrance with everyone staring at me. Walking into this room was my least favourite thing to do—I hated it even more than picking up poo, not that I'd ever had to, but still, I could imagine how gross picking up poo after your dog was, and I'd do that a hundred times if it meant I didn't have to walk in here and be eyeballed by judgemental witches.

I stepped around Gus and into the room. Everyone turned to look at me, of course, and my heart rate kicked up. Drake sat at the head of the table, Ma'am to his left, Dana to his right, and Will next to her. James and Millicent sat on the other side of Ma'am; then there was a spare seat and Beren. Two more agents I didn't know—a middle-aged man and woman—sat next to Will. It was pretty much a full house.

Drake gave me a nod. "Thank you for joining us, Miss Bianchi. Please take a seat."

I hurried to sit next to Millicent, as they were obviously waiting for me before they started the meeting, or maybe they weren't. Maybe they'd had some of the meeting—the part I wasn't supposed to hear. Whatever. I shouldn't be offended—I didn't want to be an agent after all, but I hated that Dana thought that made her superior. I risked a glance her way, but she was already ignoring me, her gaze on Drake. Someone else did meet my eyes, however.

Will.

My cheeks heated. He'd caught my gaze, and I couldn't look away. The shock of him actually noticing me had me like a deer in headlights. What were those blue-grey eyes trying to tell me? He didn't smile, didn't frown, just stared. I swatted away the butterflies in my stomach. *I don't like you. I don't like you.*

Drake stood, and I turned my attention to him. If Will wanted to say something to me, he could have come to Angelica's place at any time. Whatever this staring thing was, I was not buying in.

Drake straightened his lemon-yellow tie. "As you all know, the situation in Kent, and more specifically, Westerham, is volatile. With the number of crimes escalating sharply, the police were understaffed. That situation has become even more critical with the sidelining of a number of officers who have also been affected by whatever this is. We're doing all we can, but it's clear at this stage, it's not enough." He stepped away from his chair. He clasped his hands behind his back and strolled along behind Dana, Will, and the two other agents I didn't know. "Whilst the frequency of violence has diminished since yesterday, we can surmise that it's because so many people were already locked up. But those who were arrested up to this time yesterday have calmed down. We and the police have released many of them, as they were first-time offenders, and we need to clear space for new arrests. My worry is that whatever set them off will reoccur."

I resisted an eye-roll. Yeah, you and everyone else in this

room. It would be great if he could tell us something we didn't know.

He turned and sauntered his way back towards his chair. "So, what are we to do, you may ask? I'll let Agent DuPree Senior explain what I managed to arrange with my mates from the army and Kent Police." He gave Ma'am a nod and sat in his chair. Wow, way to take all the credit, duck man. I couldn't deal with his crap on a daily basis. I'd do something to get arrested pretty quickly if he were my boss. It was a good thing I didn't have my heart set on joining the PIB.

"Thank you, Agent Pembleton." Angelica gave him a cool smile, then stood. "As the affected people come to their senses, we're interviewing them about their movements in the twenty-four hours prior to becoming violent. The blood tests are clear of viruses. Also, because of the consistent duration of the violence in each person as well as the fact that family members or friends aren't always affected, we're ruling out a virus. Our summation is that we're dealing with contaminated food or drink, but we haven't found any traces of magic on the sufferers. If we find that this is indeed a malicious attack on the citizens of Kent, we will drop all charges against those affected. They become victims rather than perpetrators."

I thought about the old guy who had attacked me and my bananas. He'd had to pay for them. I put up my hand. "Excuse me, Ma'am."

"Yes, Lily."

"If the perpetrators are caught, does that mean they're liable for any damages payable or murders, etcetera?" It was unfair that the old guy was out of pocket, and it hadn't even been his fault.

Agent Laaam turned to me and rolled her eyes, as if I'd asked an obvious question that any idiot would know the answer to. I gave her a bland look. I was not going to bite.

Ma'am answered, "Yes. That is correct."

"Thanks." Wow, what a mess it was going to be when this was all over. Whoever had done this stood to be accused of hundreds, if not thousands, of crimes. They could probably make it into the *Guinness Book of World Records* for most charges against a criminal. Not the record you wanted to be breaking, although, I bet serial killers always hoped they would be the winner for most murders. Sickos.

Ma'am continued. "The army has deployed soldiers into Westerham and other villages. They'll patrol the high street and surrounding blocks. We're also enforcing a 9:00 p.m. to 5:00 a.m. curfew. It will probably take a few more days until we've narrowed down the specific food or beverage responsible—we have a mountain of information to get through."

I put my hand up again.

"Yes, Lily?"

Dana sighed loudly. I pretended she wasn't there.

"Couldn't it be more than one thing? What if it's a bakery, for instance, and they've contaminated all their products?"

Ma'am nodded. "If that's the case, we'll close in on them quicker. Everyone affected will have eaten from the same place."

Dana rolled her eyes again. "Honestly, Lily. Can you ask something that the rest of us don't know the answer to?"

My cheeks heated as everyone turned to stare at me. Were they all thinking the same thing? I risked making a bigger idiot of myself, but I wasn't going to let her insult go unchallenged. "But what if that bakery wasn't a small local bakery, but a large bakery that delivered to all the stores and cafés?"

Dana huffed. "We'd still get to the bottom of it. Honestly, I don't even know what you're doing here. You're as useless as a non-witch. In fact, isn't it true that we waste precious PIB resources covering your arse?"

I tried to ignore the burst of adrenaline flooding my body and took a slow breath. How did she know? And did she know why? Probably not, or she would have just come right out with it. And why was everyone staying silent?

Willing my voice to come out strong and even, I said, "I didn't ask for anyone to protect me. What's it to you, anyway? Why do you hate me so much? You've been nothing but awful to me since the day I met you."

She laughed and pointed to herself. "Who, me? I'm nothing but nice to everyone. I think you're just jealous because I have everything you want. If I point out your shortcomings, it's only because I'm passionate about protecting the PIB and my fellow agents from incompetence."

The more everyone else stayed quiet, the more unsettled I became. Ma'am's face was sympathetic, as if to say, "I'm sorry, but she's right. I just didn't have the heart to break it to you." James wore an expression of mild surprise, Beren and William were shaking their heads, and the two agents I didn't know were giving each other looks as if they were extremely uncomfortable and didn't know where else to look. I turned to Millicent, and she shrugged. Shrugged! Had everyone abandoned me?

Dana turned to Drake. "I think we should ask her to leave, sir. She's slowing us down, and quite frankly, she shouldn't be privy to classified PIB information. And I don't see why the PIB should be guarding her either. It's time she fended for herself. If she hasn't learned enough magic to look after herself by now, bad luck."

He cleared his throat and considered her request. "Yes, yes, Agent Lam. I think you're right." He turned to Angelica. "Please desist on providing Lily with a protection detail."

Ma'am nodded, her expression blank. "Consider it done."

What the hell? She hadn't even hesitated. I knew she was acting weird and wasn't herself, but a little piece of my heart still broke off and fell into the growing abyss inside me.

The duck turned his stern gaze my way. "Please leave, Lily. You're no longer permitted on the PIB premises."

My mouth dropped open. Seriously? I mean, I should be happy, since I didn't like being here anyway, but I hated being forced into anything. And whilst I knew Dana was probably using her powers of persuasion on everyone—because how else could this make sense—I had to bite my tongue to stop tears from escaping. Everyone I cared about was turning their back on me. Is this what they'd thought about me all along? And how was she hiding the fact that she was using her magic? There were no telltale tingles or warmth on my scalp or skin. Then I remembered that using your talent didn't necessarily mean anyone else would sense it. If you were only using your inherent power, not drawing from the golden river, no one would know. But if she were using her talent on that many people simultaneously, surely she would need to draw extra power? Or was she the strongest witch ever? Crap.

My original feelings of dislike for her fed on her spiteful words and on the continued silence of those who should have been defending me. Dislike contorted into hate. Now that my heart had been hollowed out, left to collapse without the support and love of those I trusted, I had nothing to lose. Stuff her and her threats—even if she was super strong and could probably kill me with a point of a finger.

I pushed my chair back and stood, careful to appear composed and rational, not lost and vulnerable like I really was. Back straight, I shook my head, willing my jelly-like legs to stay strong and not collapse. "You've all been fooled by Dana. She's using her powers of persuasion on you all. She's the one who isn't fit to be here, using her 'talent' when it's forbidden. And you're all too bewitched to see it."

Dana narrowed her eyes and gave me a small shake of her head. Then she looked past me to Millicent and smirked. Oh, crap. Was she going to make good on her earlier threat?

Millicent groaned. I spun around. She sat clutching her stomach, her face whiter than usual. James jumped out of his seat and knelt in front of her. "What is it, Mill?" His wide eyes stared into hers.

"Bad... cramp." She was breathing heavily. "I need to get to the doctor." Her eyes shut, and she scrunched her face.

Dana tsked. "Now see what you've done, Lily. You're bad news. If Millicent loses her baby, it will be all your fault." Dana's dark eyes were damn near black as she stared at me, accusing and victorious.

Ma'am, Beren, and Will shook their heads at me. James and Millicent had no mind for anyone else—whatever was happening with the baby had their full attention.

"We're going to the hospital. Beren, please come with us," James said before he swept Millicent into his arms and disappeared. Beren stood and stepped through his doorway. I had no idea how he knew which hospital to go to. Maybe they had an emergency plan in place since he was the best healer the PIB had?

Drake scowled at me. It was clear I wasn't welcome anymore, not to mention it was my fault Millicent's baby was in danger. It was time for me to go, but Dana hadn't won. No one hurt those I loved and got away with it. She could've asked Snezana how kidnapping James had gone... if Snezana had still been alive.

I fought the urge to jump across the table and break

Dana's nose. Instead, I gave her my most serene smile and dredged confidence up from somewhere down deep. "If anything happens to Millicent's baby, I'll be coming for you."

She laughed, her bright-red lips revealing her glowing-white teeth.

"Your adolescent magic is no competition for my power and experience. Now run along home, child, and leave the grown-ups to their work."

I had to hand it to her—her talent was impressive. Everyone was watching our exchange without a hint of incredulousness at such a petty argument in the middle of a meeting. No one said a word. Funny that her powers hadn't worked on me. Surely it would have been easier to brain-wash me than force the issue this way? Wow, how hadn't I seen that before? My smile, this time, was genuine. "You *should* be afraid of me, Agent Laaam. How many other people are immune to your talent? I'm guessing no one. Does it make you wonder what else I'm capable of?"

Her glee disappeared. She gripped both chair arms. Anger pulsed from her, but she didn't say anything. I thought so. It must be time to go.

I gave her a wave. Before I could tell myself what a stupid idea it was, I made my doorway around myself, the way Angelica did, the way Dana had said I would never master. My heart raced as I waited for the pain of a chopped off foot or scalp—it was impossible to see what you were doing and where to create the edges of the doorway when it wasn't in front of you.

A moment of familiar warmth travelled from my head to my neck and shoulders, and I was standing in Ma'am's reception room. I'd done it! Ha, take that, Witchface. My happiness was short-lived, unfortunately, when I remembered Millicent and the baby. God, I hoped evil Dana hadn't hurt the baby.

Nausea gripped my insides, and my mouth went dry. I needed to find out which hospital James had taken Millicent to and get myself over there. Hopefully they didn't blame me for what happened, but if they were under Dana's spell, they likely hated me.

It was a chance I had to take. I pulled out my phone and texted James. *Are Millicent and the baby okay? Can I come and see you?*

I stared at the screen for a minute, blood pounding past my ears, waiting for an answer. But none came. I hung my head and closed my eyes. *Please be okay.*

I unlocked the reception-room door and stepped into the hall before locking the door again. Should I ask Olivia for help? My eyes burned with tears. I had no one else to turn to. Guilt constricted my throat, making it hard to breathe. If it wasn't for my stupid pride, Millicent and the baby would be fine. Why did I have to goad the piranha? But then, what if no one ever stood up to her? She'd be ruling the world with her horrible brand of evil before everyone knew it.

I unlocked my phone and stared at the screen. Nothing. Maybe I should text Beren? Was he as angry at me as James and Millicent probably were? Would he be in the middle of healing Millicent? My interruption wouldn't be welcome and might distract him. I took a shaky breath and blew it out. I typed one last message to James. If he didn't get back to me, there was nothing I could do except give him space.

Hey. I'm so sorry about what happened at the meeting. I didn't mean to put Millicent or the baby in danger. I hope you can both forgive me. It would break my heart if anything happened to them. Please let Millicent know I send my love, and I understand if you don't want to talk to me right now. Even if you hate me, please let me know how they are when you know something. Xx.

I wiped moisture from my eyes and sniffed. There was no use doing nothing all day and pining for a message. Even though I wasn't wanted at the PIB, there were still people out there who needed this mystery to be solved. So many people's lives would be ruined if the violence continued. And how many people would die for nothing? And why did Piranha want me gone from the investigation? Did she stand to gain from solving it or from the continuation of violence?

Yikes. Was I onto something? Maybe I just had an over-active imagination. But how would she gain if Westerham imploded? No, that was ridiculous. She just wanted the glory, and she hated that Will and I had been friends, and yeah, she could tell I liked him.

I wasn't sure if Olivia was home or even if she was still asleep after getting back late last night, but I needed a friend, and I was sure she'd want to help figure out what was going on.

I went upstairs and knocked on her door.

"Come in."

Thank God she was there. Some of the heaviness lifted from my chest, and I opened the door. She was dressed and sitting at her desk. She turned around. "Hey, Lily." Her smile flatlined. "What's wrong?" She stood and came over to me.

Gah, I didn't want to cry, but just the simple act of her asking what was wrong, caring, brought the burn of tears. I bit the inside of my cheek to stop from losing it altogether. "Um." Where to start? "Millicent was having stomach cramps in the PIB meeting, and James rushed her to hospital. Oh, and everyone hates me." That about covered it.

She wrapped her hand around my upper arm. "Is she okay? When did this happen?"

"About fifteen minutes ago. I've texted James, but he hasn't answered. Beren went with them, but I didn't want to bother him in case he was healing her. I don't know if they haven't answered me because they hate me or if they're still figuring out what's wrong with Millicent."

She hugged me. "Oh, honey. I'm so sorry." She released me, and her forehead scrunched. "But why would they hate you? No one hates you."

I told her about Dana's threats the other day, and then about everything that happened at the meeting. Her eyes got wider as I told her the story; then her mouth dropped open. By the time I finished, her jaw was clenched, and anger leeched from her like petrol fumes ready to ignite.

"I mean, I know I shouldn't have goaded her like that, but, argh... I'm so bad at stopping myself. Now Millicent could lose the baby because I'm such an idiot."

She shook her head. "No freaking way. It is not your fault. She's a psychopath. She's the one who hurt Millicent, not you. If everyone wasn't under her influence, they'd totally be on your side. We have to figure out a way to expose what she's doing. From what you've told me, and the things I've been learning from the secret PIB part of the police-training course, what she's doing is illegal. She'll go to jail. Angelica is going to be ropeable when she finds out."

"*If* she finds out." I couldn't help thinking things were going to get worse before they got better, but Liv had a point. Angelica wouldn't take too kindly to being made a fool of. "Using a talent can be done quietly, as in, other witches don't notice anything. I have no idea how to prove anything." My shoulders slumped. "What am I doing, going against her? Am I crazy?"

"It's true that it seems unbelievable that Dana would dare tamper with Angelica's mind, but Angelica's always had your back, so has Beren, and your brother and Millicent love you. Even stupid Will cares about you—"

I opened my mouth to dispute Will giving a crap, but Liv put her hand against my lips.

"I don't know what's going on with him, but he cares. Maybe there's another reason he's acting the way he is. Have you ever thought of that?"

Of course I'd hoped there was another reason, but I figured it was wishful thinking. I shrugged. "But what?"

"We're just going to have to find out. I'm here for you, Lil. We'll sort out this mess together, and we'll figure out what's going on in Westerham. By the time we're finished with Witchface, she'll regret ever meeting you." Olivia's grin promised that Piranha was going to pay, big time.

"You're the best friend ever. Thanks, Liv." I gave her a hug.

"I know." She snickered. "So, why don't we get started?"

I smiled. "Yes, let's."

CHAPTER 4

Now that we were trying to solve this together, Olivia was keener on asking her mum about her friend. She managed to get the lady's number only after promising not to tell her exactly what her mother had done. She agreed to only say that her mother had been unwell. Although, if this woman was the normal tight-lipped English person, she might not want to talk to us about her experience. But we wouldn't pry too much. We just needed to confirm she hadn't been herself, and then we could check out the teahouse.

Thankfully, she agreed to meet with us. Her house was a cute semi-detached brick cottage of two stories with white sash windows and a sloping red-tiled roof. There was no driveway, so we parked on the street. As we reached her front door, barking erupted from inside.

"Maggie, Molly, hush." The door opened. A tall, thin

woman who must have been in her fifties stood holding one white Maltese terrier in each arm. Her brown hair was tied back in a loose ponytail, and she wore faded blue jeans and a white short-sleeved shirt. "Olivia, darling!" She smiled. "It's so good to see you. It's been too long. You look wonderful."

Olivia smiled. "Thanks, Mrs Fleming."

"Oh, call me Joan. You're too old to be calling me Mrs Fleming. Please come in." She stepped aside.

"Old habits die hard." Olivia smiled and went in before me. When I crossed the threshold, she said, "This is my friend, Lily."

I smiled at Mrs Fleming. "Lovely to meet you, Mrs Fleming. Thank you so much for agreeing to talk to us about yesterday."

Her smile faded. She shut the door and walked down the hallway and into a low-ceilinged living room. Well, I'd certainly killed the friendly mood. Unfortunately, there was no way to skirt around why we were there. What if she changed her mind about opening up to us?

"Please sit down." She indicated a cream leather three-seat couch. "Can I get either of you a cup of tea or something else to drink?"

Olivia's smile was gentle. "No, we're fine, thanks. If you want to grab something, we'll wait."

"No, that's okay. I suppose we'd best get this over with." She sat in the single-seat plush chair that matched the couch and shifted both dogs into her lap. "What would you like to know?"

I was going to let Olivia start this off—Mrs Fleming obviously felt more comfortable talking to her. "I know you had morning tea with Mum two days ago. She was rather… unwell that afternoon, and I was wondering if maybe you hadn't felt yourself either?"

Mrs Fleming rested both hands on the dogs' backs and massaged them. "In what way?"

I held in a sigh. This was going to be harder than I thought. I looked at Olivia, seeking direction. She knew this woman—I didn't. Olivia gave me a nod, which I interpreted as a "you can talk."

"Well, Mrs Fleming—"

"Please call me Joan, Lily. We're informal around here." She tittered what must be her nervous laugh.

"Have you watched the local news over the last couple of days?" Asking a question was a more subtle way to get to the point without having to ask something direct and confronting.

"Yes. It's been horrible. I haven't left the house since that afternoon. Everyone's going crazy. It's just not safe anymore."

"We"—I glanced at Olivia, then back to Joan—"believe that someone's put masses of hormones into the water or food here, you know, like those weightlifters who have too many steroids?"

She blinked a few times. "Oh, you think people have been having 'roid rage?"

"Yes, exactly. All the terrible things people are doing aren't actually their fault." I smiled. "I'm so sorry to ask you, but we're trying to catch those responsible. If we find them, they'll be held accountable for everything." She had stopped massaging the dogs and was gripping their fur, likely holding on for dear life. I wasn't sure I'd done enough, but we couldn't avoid the question all day. I made my expression as gentle as possible. "Were you unusually angry that afternoon or evening?"

One of the dogs yelped—she must have gripped a tad too hard. "Oh, darling, I'm so sorry." She rubbed the dog's back and kept looking at him, or was it her, while she answered. "Yes, I was. I live alone—well, not alone, alone, but my husband passed away last year. The dogs were asleep in their beds, thank goodness, because if they hadn't been, I have no idea what they might have done to upset me, and then I might have hurt them. There's no way I could live with myself if I did that." She lifted one of the dogs off her lap and squished it in a hug and then sat it back on her lap again. "I did receive a phone call from the man who mows my lawns, letting me know he couldn't make it that day. Well, I just got so angry. I couldn't even think. I just yelled and screamed at him and told him never to come back. I even swore at him." She looked surprised, even now, as if she couldn't believe she'd done it.

Olivia turned to me. "Joan never swears. Neither does my mum. I don't think I've ever heard either of them swear." I wasn't sure if Olivia was trying to convince me or make Joan feel better.

"You definitely don't look like the sort of person who

swears, Joan. It sounds as if you were affected, just like everyone else."

She nodded. "It sounds like it, but that's not the worst of it, I'm afraid." She took a couple of deep breaths. "I'm ashamed of what happened next, well, all of it, really, but this.... If Leonard had been alive to see my behaviour, he would have been horrified."

"It's okay. We won't judge you. You're helping so many people by telling us this, and we won't tell anyone else what you tell us." And I wouldn't. This was just Olivia and me. I didn't owe the PIB anything, except maybe a punch in the guts to one particular agent.

"Well, I hung up on Mr Finch, the lawn man. Then I slammed the phone on the table and woke the dogs. Then I spied my teacup on the table, and I just… I just picked it up and smashed it against the wall." The poor woman shook her head, unable to come to terms with what she'd done. "I imagined the wall was Mr Finch's head. If he'd been here, I hate to think what I would have done to him. I wasn't in control of myself." She turned her gaze on Olivia. "What if it happens again, Liv? What if I hurt my dogs?" Her eyes shone with tears.

Olivia stood and went to Joan, then knelt on the floor next to her chair and held her hand. "It happened to me too. I know how you feel. I haven't had another episode, but there's no telling when or if it will happen again. That's why talking to you today was so important. Did you go anywhere else before or after morning tea?"

"I stopped at the supermarket and bought biscuits and milk, but that's it."

"Did you eat the biscuits that day or drink the milk?" I asked.

"No. I opened them this morning. I feel fine right now. But didn't you say it was the water?"

"It might be the water, but it might be some other kind of food or drink that half of Westerham have consumed. It might even be more than one kind of food. So you didn't go to a bakery or anything?"

She shook her head. "So is my milk safe to drink?" She sat up straight and stared at me, obviously desperate for my answer.

"I think so, considering you've had some today and you feel fine. Do you mind if I have a look at them? Maybe I can check."

Olivia stood and turned to look at me. As Joan shooed the dogs off her lap and stood, Olivia whispered to me, "Do you really think you can tell?"

I shrugged. "Maybe." Hmm, if a witch had done this— and I couldn't imagine any other explanation—there should be the hint of magic or a magic signature somewhere, surely. The magic might fade once it had been through someone's digestive tract, or what had Angelica suggested? That the magic was in the food rather than the person, that the food or drink or whatever it was affected the person in its altered state, rather than the magic. Gah, my head hurt. This was so confusing.

Joan led us to the kitchen and took out the packet of

biscuits and carton of milk. I called up my other sight. Nothing. Biscuits and milk had no aura. They just looked dead. No energy came off them. I picked up the biscuits and sniffed them, then flipped open the top of the milk carton and did the same—I couldn't exactly tell her I was a witch, and I was looking at them through another plane.

I put them back on the counter. "I can't smell anything unusual. They seem fine to me."

"What about the tap water? Can you check that please?"

Oh, dear, I'd created a monster. She was going to question everything edible in the house. Although, that wasn't such a bad idea. It wouldn't hurt to be thorough. I turned on the tap and looked at the water. I smiled. Silver and gold flecks glinted as the water ran into the sink. Wow. Was that because water contained living organisms? Or was it traces of magic from the source? It certainly didn't look sinister, and if it had been the water supply, everyone would have been affected. I leant over and sniffed at the stream— keeping up appearances.

I turned off the tap. "It's all good. What else would you like me to look at?"

We went through the fruit bowl first, then her tea bags, then the vegetables and butter in her fridge. Lastly, I sniffed the half a loaf of bread in the bread bin. "All clear. I'm thinking it's probably something you ate or drank at the teahouse."

Her mouth dropped open. "I can't stop drinking tea!"

"You won't have to. Just don't go there for a while. And I've checked your tea here, so you're free to drink that."

"All right. Thank you, girls. You've been so helpful. I feel much better now."

"If anything happens, though, please let us know. Take notice of where you buy things, and if you have another episode, call Olivia, and we'll come right over."

She didn't look too happy about the prospect of a reoccurrence, but she nodded. "I will. Thank you again."

She showed us out, and Olivia gave her a parting hug. We got in Olivia's car, and I turned to her. "You didn't drink or eat at that teahouse; did you?"

"No, but Mum did, and that was the only thing they'd both done that day."

"If only we had access to all the interviews the police and the PIB conducted. I suppose they'll sort it out. If there's a pattern, they'll find it. They have way more resources than we do." Disappointment slid its ginormous bottom onto my happy place and squashed it. But did it really matter who figured out the culprit as long as someone did, and soon? My ego could handle not being the one.

But what if Dana was trying to hinder the investigation? I just couldn't work out why. "Liv? What reason could Dana have for wanting to delay fixing this mess? I've wracked my brain, but I can't think of anything except she wants to be the one to crack it and get the credit."

"Hmm. Maybe she's not trying to hinder the investigation. Maybe she just wanted you gone, and now she's achieved that, the PIB will work things out quickly?"

"Maybe, but let's not count on it. I have a gut feeling this is going to drag on for a while."

"Well, then, we'd better keep going. Where do you want to go now?"

"I guess we should go to that teahouse, check it out, maybe buy what they had and take it home, see if I can figure out if it's tainted somehow."

Olivia bit her lip and stared out the windscreen for a moment. Then she turned to me. "I could be the tester. I could have a little bit and see what happens."

"Oh my God, no! No way, Liv. I'm not putting you through that again, or me. Plus, I need you to help me investigate. There's not much we can do if you're out of it for twenty-four hours."

"So how are you going to see if it's tainted?"

"The same way I checked out Mrs Fleming's food—I'll use my other sight."

"How do you know it works? You didn't see anything weird just then."

"True." I worried my bottom lip between my teeth. We had to start somewhere, though. "Look, I'm not sure if I'll be able to see anything, but we may as well give it a try. The food may not even be tainted today. What if it was a one-day thing?"

A shrill scream came from across the street. I jerked my head to look past Olivia and through her window. A large man was dragging a woman along the footpath, her long red hair gripped in his hand. She was bent at the waist and running to keep up with him. "Help! Help!"

Crap.

He was at least six foot and beefy. Even though he

looked like half fat, half muscle, he could pulverise me and her at the same time with little effort. I couldn't let him keep hurting her, but what could I do?

I jumped out of the car and crossed the road, Liv's worried voice following me. "Get back in the car, Lily."

I looked back over my shoulder. "I can't, Liv. But don't worry. I'll be fine." Whatever I was going to do, I'd better figure it out. Maybe distraction would work for a bit? "Hey, boofhead! Moron!"

He stopped and turned. His enraged stare locked on me. My heart hammered, and the rational part of my brain begged me to turn around and get back in the car. But there was no way I was leaving this woman to get beaten and maybe killed. She'd gripped her own hair with one hand and was trying to back out of his hold as she sobbed.

"What did you say?"

"I said you're a boofhead and a moron." My legs trembled. They wanted to collapse, but I wouldn't let them. "I've called the police. They'll be here in a minute. Let her go."

"Make me, cow." He yanked her hair, and she flew towards him. Her knees slammed into the concrete. She screamed. Jesus. This had to end now.

I imagined the golden river of power. I knew I wasn't supposed to use it on non-witches, but this was an emergency. If I ended up in jail for this, so be it. I whispered, "Make this violent man in front of me release his captive, then buzz out his anger like a giant bumblebee." Hmm, I had not seen that coming. The things my brain came up with….

He released the woman's hair, stared at his offending hand, then stared at me. He clenched his jaw and shook his head. "No!" he shouted as his hands came to his waist, his arms forming triangles or bee's wings. "Bzzz, bzzz, bzzz," he said and flapped his arms back and forth. I snorted. His gaze darted around and landed on the flowers in a garden two doors down from where he stood. He buzzed again and flitted over to them on tiptoes. When he got there, he dropped to his knees and shoved his nose into the happy yellow petals.

The woman sat up and looked around. I went to her and helped her stand. Her cheeks were wet with tears, and snot coated the space between nostrils and mouth. She rubbed her head with one hand and wiped her nose with the other. "What just happened?"

I couldn't really answer that question, so I asked one of my own. "Do you want me to take you to the hospital or the police?"

"I think I'm okay. Brian's never been violent before. I don't know what got into him." She shuddered and took a shaky breath.

"When did it start?"

"About an hour ago, I think."

I wasn't about to let an opportunity go. "What has he eaten and drunk today?"

"He had sausages, toast, and a cup of tea for breakfast. That's it, I think."

"At home or out?"

"Why are you asking me these questions?"

"I've heard the police think there's something in the food. Please just tell me where you got the food. You don't want this to happen again, do you?"

She looked over at Brian, who had his head in a rose bush. "Um, we got the sausages from the Westerham butcher, and the tea I get from T-riffic. They can make up whatever blend you want. But we've never had a problem with them before. And I made the bread with supermarket-bought flour."

"Okay, thanks. I appreciate your help."

"Will he be okay? I mean, should I watch him, make sure he's all right?"

He straightened from the roses and zigzagged to the next house, buzzing as he went. "Um, I guess you could watch him. He'll probably be a bit confused when it wears off."

"Okay, thanks, um, what was your name?"

I smiled. "Lily."

"Thanks for helping me. I just…. He's not usually—"

"I know, but if it happens again, please call the police."

She nodded and slowly followed Brian as he buzzed from flower to flower. I smirked, then went back to the car.

When I'd gotten in and shut the door, Olivia asked, "What the hell just happened? What did you do?"

"Nothing. Absolutely nothing. It's illegal for a witch to put a spell on a non-witch, even if it's to save his girlfriend or sister or whoever she is and stop his violent rampage. Maybe he just decided to channel his energy into *bee*-ing more productive?" I snorted.

"That was rather bzzz-arre." She giggled and started the car. "To the teahouse?"

"Yes, and afterwards we'll take a detour to T-riffic. Have you heard of it?"

"I have, actually. I sometimes get tea from there. They have the most amazing blends." She signalled, looked over her shoulder, then pulled out.

The teahouse was only a few minutes down the road, on the fringe of Westerham. Olivia pulled into a reasonable-sized dirt parking area that sprawled in front of a two-storey brick barn conversion. On the left, as we faced the building, was the teahouse, and on the right-hand side was an antique and collectables shop.

But something wasn't right. I scanned the parking area. It was almost empty. "Is this normally a popular place?"

"Yes." Olivia turned her head, looking out her window, my window, then at the large glass door directly in front. "Oh, it's closed."

Damn. "Maybe they didn't feel safe, so they shut it until things die down? Let's have a look anyway." I was reaching for my door handle when my phone dinged with a message. I hurried to get it out of my pocket, expecting or hoping to see James's number. Nope. I frowned as sadness rested heavy hands on my shoulders.

Unknown number.

I opened the message. "What the…?"

"What is it?" Olivia looked at me.

I was just about to tell her when I realised that I needed to be extra careful now that Dana had turned everyone against me. She wanted to discover my secrets, and I wouldn't put it past her to spy somehow. I whispered the private bubble spell, which meant no one else could hear our conversation with normal hearing or magic. If I was being targeted by an agent, I needed to start thinking like one.

"It's from James, but it's not from his phone. I'll read it out." I was relieved he'd messaged, and I smiled, but why hadn't he sent it from his phone? "Hey, sis, sorry I couldn't get back to you sooner. Mill and the baby are fine. The doctors said it might just be stress. Beren couldn't find anything untoward either, so we've just come home, and Mill is supposed to rest for the afternoon. I'm going to stay with her."

"That's a relief."

"I'll say, but hang on; there's more. 'I'm sending this from a throwaway phone. My other phone is being monitored. I'm not sure what happened this afternoon, Lil, but I want you to know that I know Dana is up to something. Everyone was acting weird, so I thought I'd better play along, but I've got your back. I'm sorry I had to pretend like I didn't notice. Also, the emergency with Millicent. It's not safe for us to catch up today, but I'll try and work something out for tomorrow, and bring Olivia. Also, just so you know it's me: Mum's diaries. Love you. J.'"

I lifted my head and met Olivia's stare. She smiled. "Told you he'd be on your side. What the hell is going on over there? And if Dana's managed to influence everyone else, how come your brother isn't affected?"

"Probably the same reason she can't influence me. Maybe it's some kind of genetic talent?"

"Don't look at me. I know even less than you do." She grinned.

"That's not something to be happy about. Sheesh. We need all the info we can get." I smiled. It did feel good to know my brother still loved me. And now, if we found anything, I could pass the information onto him. "We've still got work to do. Let's go."

I slid out of the car and approached the front doors. I rested my forehead on the glass and peered in. Empty chairs sat at clean tables. The lights were off, although daylight gave me a clear view of the unmanned register and the vacant display windows next to the counter that normally would have held ready-made food.

Olivia stood next to me and looked in. After a couple of minutes, we stepped back. "Now what?" she asked.

"Well, we can't get any samples to test, which is really disappointing. If I knew where they kept their tea, I could magic some out, but without being able to visualise it…" I shrugged. "What if we go to the hospital? It's not like they can close. We'll get a sample of whatever you had."

"Yeah, but Dad ate there too, and he was fine."

"True. You both had the pudding, right?"

"Yes, although we drank different things."

"I thought you both had tea?"

"I had Earl Grey, and he had English Breakfast." Her eyes grew bigger as she likely realised what that meant.

It was kind of exciting news. It meant that maybe only

one type of tea was affected—if, indeed, tea was the culprit. Considering most English people drank tea, it would make sense to contaminate it if you wanted to create a massive calamity. Putting poison or whatever in the water supply was probably a tad too obvious and trickier.

I grinned. "Come on. Let's go." I hurried to her car and jumped in. Excitement had my legs bouncing.

My happy buzz was short-lived.

The prickly sensation of someone using magic crawled from my scalp down my nape. I shuddered. Normally, it was just a warm, slightly uncomfortable feeling, but this had an ickiness about it, like the stabbing of fast-moving, little cockroach claws. As Olivia got in the car, I whispered the return-to-sender spell and tensed, waiting for the drain on my power. It didn't come, but I kept my guard up. I glanced around the car park. I was sure we'd been the only ones here. Had we been followed?

Olivia turned to me. "What's wrong?"

"There's a witch out there using magic."

"Could it just be random, like someone magicking something to themselves, and they just happen to be nearby?"

"Maybe, but I get the feeling it's more than that." There was no one near us, that I could see, anyway, but I didn't want to take any chances. It might be someone sent by whoever was after me, or it could be Dana, looking to cause more trouble. As much as it pained me to say it, I couldn't take the risk. "Liv, let's go home. I need a coffee." I shook my head at her, hoping she didn't argue. Whoever was out there could be listening in, and I didn't have the skill to keep up a return-to-sender spell and a bubble of silence. I snorted. The things I was saying to myself these days would have had the me from a few months ago thinking it was time to check myself into somewhere that had straight jackets.

"What's so funny?"

"Nothing, really."

"You can't do that, Lily."

"Huh?"

"It's like when someone on Facebook posts a vague status, like 'I'm over this,' or whatever. It's bad form, lady. Bad form."

I laughed. "Fair enough. I hate vaguebooking too. I was just musing at how weird my life is now that things like bubbles of silence and spells are the norm. How the hell did I get here?" I hadn't had that much time to ponder things since I'd arrived in the UK, and that was probably a good thing because the life I lived now was a tad terrifying. But did I want to return to ignorance and a relatively simple life back in Sydney? It was certainly tempting.

Olivia started the car. "I'm not sure how you got here, but I'm glad you made it." She smiled. "Let's get you that coffee."

As she drove out of the premises, I spied a black Porsche across the road. The windows were so dark that I couldn't see who was inside. "Pull over for a sec."

Liv did as I asked.

I took out my phone, then leant across to whisper in her ear. "See that Porsche? What's the number plate?" She had a better view of it than I did, and I wasn't going to get out of the car and be obvious about what I was doing. I also hoped if they were listening in with magic, that they couldn't hear a whisper. I was pretty sure listening with magic was like having a listening device that didn't necessarily amplify what was being said.

I handed her my phone, and she typed in the seven letter-number combination.

"Thanks. Okay, let's go."

We didn't talk on the way back to Angelica's. As soon as we arrived home and got inside, I dropped my return-to-sender spell and made a bubble of silence around the two of us. Dana had influenced Angelica, so there was no way I wanted her hearing what I had to say either. Guilt sat uncomfortably in my chest like heartburn. Angelica had been my mother's best friend, and she'd protected me so far, but things had changed. I knew it wasn't real—if Dana hadn't tampered with her mind, I wouldn't be in this situation. But she had, and I was. It didn't mean I had to like keeping secrets from Angelica.

We went into the kitchen. I turned the coffee machine on, and Olivia filled the kettle. Then we sat next to each other at the kitchen table.

"It's safe to talk. I've created a bubble. I couldn't before because I had another spell activated."

"Okay, cool. So, why the change of plans?" Olivia asked.

"We'd been followed by, I'm guessing, whoever was in the Porsche. Now that I'm blacklisted from the PIB, I have to be extra careful. They took my protective detail away too."

Her mouth formed a large *O*. "Oh my God! You didn't mention that before. Surely James wouldn't leave you vulnerable?"

"Ordinarily, no, but stupid Piranha's influenced everyone. I bet if James asked an agent to watch over me, they'd say no, that they've had orders from higher up. Dana questioned the fact that resources were being wasted on me, and she had everyone's support. Even Beren and William are caught up in her magic." Another piece of my heart broke off and slid into the ever-deepening black hole of abandonment. I took a moment to feel sorry for myself. Dramatic, I knew, but totally justified.

"You're not on your own." Olivia put her hand on mine. "I know I can't do magic, but I've got your back. Whatever you need, just ask."

"Thanks, Liv. I appreciate it." Boiling water echoed inside the steel kettle and tripped the off switch. *Click.*

Olivia made her tea while I manually made my coffee—I wasn't done with my bubble of silence yet.

Once we had our beverages, we reconvened at the table. I deeply inhaled the heady coffee scent. It did wonders to soothe my angst. If only coffee could solve all my problems.

I took a sip, then spoke. "I have the makings of a plan."

"Spill."

"Okay, so I need the address of that hospital and exactly which cafeteria it is because they sometimes have more than one."

She nodded. "I can do that. What else?"

"Once you give me that, I can look up the coordinates on my mind map and travel there, grab the samples we need, and come back. In the meantime, I'm hoping you can look up the number plate. Do you know how to access those things yet?"

"I know where I'm supposed to get the information, but I need to be added to the system first, as in, I need to have an authorised account."

"Hmm. I could probably magic you in somehow, but if we got caught, we'd both be in a world of crap. I wonder if James could arrange it without being found out?"

"It's worth a try."

"The only problem is that I have to wait for him to contact me. We may have to wait a day or two for that, but I can grab those samples today and start testing."

Olivia curled both hands around her cup. "Sounds good. Then what?"

"Well, it depends on the results. If I can't figure anything out, we're back to the beginning, but if I get a positive result, we'll have to find out where they get their tea from. The number of people affected means it's probably not individuals at different places contaminating the tea. It's likely happening at the source."

"True. So, if Angelica comes home when you're out, what do you want me to say?"

I tapped my fingernail against my mug. She was sure to know if Olivia lied. "I hate saying this, but we can't trust her, and she can read your mind if she wants. She'll know if you're not telling the truth. I could put a mind shield on you, but then she'd just be suspicious. I can't risk anything getting back to the psycho fish."

Olivia giggled. "Wouldn't it be cool if you could turn her into an actual piranha. Then we could flush her down the toilet."

I laughed. "I couldn't think of anything more fitting. I'll get started on that spell once we figure out who's ruining Westerham society." It was good to have goals.

"So what can you do to make sure Angelica doesn't find out what we're doing?"

"I wonder if I could protect just the thoughts to do with me and disguise it so no one can tell at a quick look. It's illegal for witches to read minds without due cause, but now Dana's involved, I'd say the usual rules don't apply. But I'm thinking if anyone delves into your thoughts, it will be just a cursory look. Although, because it is illegal, Angelica's unlikely to ask me why your mind is shielded since she'll be giving herself away. I'd just rather no one figured we were being extra careful."

She shivered. "I don't like the sound of a witch slinking through my thoughts. Creepy."

"Yeah. It's not nice. Hang on a sec." I mumbled the words to magic the grimoire to me. Will had given it to me before Dana had fully gotten her sharp teeth into him. There were an insane number of spells inside. There was sure to be one for what I wanted.

I read through six pages of the contents list before I

found what I wanted: Hide Specific Thought. There was detailed information on the spell.

This spell involves burying a memory under many others. If the memory is buried deep enough, it is possible to hide it from the subjects themselves. A reverse spell may be required to give the person access to the memory at a later time. Be sure to cast the spell with only a trickle of power: the mind is a delicate thing, and you are looking to hide rather than destroy the memory. If too much force is utilised, other memories are also at risk of being destroyed. Not a spell for new witches. At least three years' experience is recommended.

I gulped and looked at Olivia, who leaned away from me.

"I don't like that look on your face, Lily. What's wrong?"

"The spell requires finesse I may not have. If I get it wrong, you'll permanently forget what I'm trying to hide, and if I'm really crap, you could lose other memories." Did I want to risk that? More importantly, did *she* want to risk it?

"Would they be memories of the last few days, because I could really stand to lose a few of those?" She grinned.

I totally knew how she felt. "I have no idea. If you don't want to do it this way, it's fine. I can just shield your mind, and so what if Angelica finds out. Although it might make you a target of Agent Witchface when she discovers you're helping me."

"If that was her following us today, she'd already realise. It's a no-brainer, really."

"Okay, we'll just go for the normal mind-protection spell."

"Cool. Let's do this." She sat up straight and licked her bottom lip.

"Don't worry. It doesn't hurt. Promise." I placed my hands on either side of her head. I was careful to only draw a small amount of power—too much would fry her brain or hair. Best not to think about that. I shook my head to clear it.

I made sure my voice was clear, confident. I didn't want Olivia worrying more than necessary. "These thoughts are Olivia's. She does not wish to share. Protect them well, little bubble, with a barrier as invisible as air." An almost inaudible bell sounded. It didn't always happen when a spell was complete, but sometimes it did. I had no idea why or what it was for, but whatever. Random witch stuff, I supposed.

"Did you hear that?"

I never would have guessed she could have heard it. "The little bell?"

"Yes. What does it mean?"

"I think it's like a confirmation the spell worked, but I really don't know for sure. See, it didn't hurt."

"No, and I don't really feel any different." She smiled and pulled out her phone. After a minute, she said, "I've got the hospital details." She opened the map, and I studied it.

I shut my eyes and brought up the world map in my mind and focussed in on Westerham. I opened my eyes and checked out the hospital in relation to where we were. I shut my eyes and adjusted the magic map in my mind, took one last look at the map on Liv's phone, and went back to the magic map. I honed in on the hospital. Once I was close enough, coordinates floated above the map. I memorised them.

"Okay, I'm off. I'll see you later."

"Don't forget: Earl Grey and English Breakfast."

"Cool. See you soon." I set the coordinates in my door and stepped through.

CHAPTER 5

The familiar hospital scent of disinfectant overlaying the faint hint of stale vomit assured me I was in the right place when I popped into the toilet cubicle. For the first time ever, I put a no-notice spell on myself and stepped out into the bathroom. Would it work? On my way to the main door, I passed a woman washing her hands. She didn't look up or acknowledge me in any way—whether I could claim victory in spell casting was another thing. Maybe she just didn't want to make eye contact with a stranger; goodness knew I tried to avoid it when I was out and about, especially in public toilets. They weren't really the place you went to meet new people.

Once out in the corridor, I looked for signs to the main entrance. Before I bought the food and drink samples, I should at least make sure I was in the right hospital. Although I shouldn't have been surprised; given what had been going on, I did a double take as I traversed the hall-ways. At various points along my route, army personnel in ruddy brown and green camouflage stood and observed. I didn't have the heart to tell them they didn't blend in against the beige walls. They were alert—not talking to each other and watching everyone. But none of them took notice of me, unless they were just experts at taking everything in without looking like it.

After a few stressful minutes, I made it to the main hospital entrance.

The letters above the doors confirmed I was in the right place. Yay for getting it right on the first try. I smiled. Now it was time to find the cafeteria. Everything was pretty clearly signposted, so it wasn't long before I was there—the mouth-watering aroma of some kind of stew confirmed it.

As I walked through the maze of metal and timber tables and chairs to the counter, the echoing clamour of a metal tray hitting the floor and plates smashing came from the left. Someone screamed, "Get off me!"

A doctor wearing scrubs hurried away from the area, as did an overweight old lady with curly grey hair. A young blonde woman in a nurse's uniform lay face down on the ground. A soldier, one knee pressing into the middle of the woman's back, was cuffing her as she thrashed. The woman shrieked unintelligibly. I cringed. The soldier got off her and dragged her up by one upper arm. The nurse was jerking, trying to get out of his grip. He pushed her, forcing her to move towards the cafeteria exit.

Her screeching faded down the hallway. I hoped that

soldier was wearing earplugs, or he was liable to end up with hearing loss.

I turned back towards the counter. The one advantage of everyone being arrested or hospitalized was that there was no line. And since this was potentially one of the ground zeroes, I imagined a lot of people who worked here or visited patients recently wouldn't be back for a while.

I stepped up to order. The dark-skinned man behind the counter was filling a steel dispenser with napkins. He didn't look up.

"Excuse me?"

Still nothing. Was he deaf? His blue turban *was* covering his ears. Maybe he couldn't hear me?

"Hello." I waved.

He finished filling the container and placed it in front of the register. Then he gazed past me, to the soldier at the door. What the hell? What was I, invisible? Oh. I laughed. *You're such an idiot.* I undid my no-notice spell.

The man started. I found it weird because I wasn't meant to be invisible. People were supposed to know I was there while not caring to look.

He blinked at me and held his hands up. "Please step back and order from there." He pointed a couple of metres behind where I was standing. He must've seen a lot of carnage in the last few days, so I didn't blame him for being wary. "Please do not come any further until it's time to pay."

I stepped back. "Is this okay?"

"Yes. What would you like?"

"Can I please get an Earl Grey tea, an English Breakfast tea, and a pudding to take away?"

"Okay."

While he made my order, I gazed around the room. The mess made by the crazed woman had been cleaned up, and there was only one person sitting at a table in the far corner. The middle-aged man intermittently stared between me and the entry as he ate. I supposed one never knew when someone else was about to go nuts. The army guy from earlier came back in and took a position just inside the cafeteria doors. Were the army members eating the food here too? Because that would spell disaster. It would make sense that they'd brought in their own food, since the PIB suspected it was food or drink contamination, and they should have passed that information onto the army.

He put my completed order on my side of the counter. "You may step forward and pay."

Oh, crap. I'd forgotten my wallet. What a ditz. I put my hand in my pocket and mumbled the spell to move my money from my wallet to my pocket. I pulled out a twenty-pound note.

"Eight pounds, please."

I handed him the note. He gave me my change, which I pocketed before grabbing the two cups of tea and the plastic container that held the pudding. Thankfully, the takeaway cups had lids, so spilling them all over me was less likely. I said my no-notice spell and made my way to the toilets. It wasn't exactly a good look to be taking food in.

Well, my first foray into gathering evidence for this case

was going well. I hoped Olivia was okay at home and that Angelica was still out. If I could prove one of these things in my hands was contaminated or spelled, we'd be one step closer to finding out who was behind this, and I so wanted to figure it out before stupid Dana.

The toilet door was in sight, just along the corridor. A slim woman attired in a white shirt and black suit walked out and turned towards me, an evil smirk on her face.

Crap. I stopped walking.

How had Dana found me? I was pretty sure there was no such thing as a tracking spell, although magic was capable of almost anything, so a spell like that could exist. But I hadn't felt her do anything to me. Is that what she'd done at the car park earlier? But I'd put my return-to-sender spell up, unless I'd been too late.

"What do we have here? A loser who loves hospital food?" She stopped in front of me. If I knew how to punch properly, I could have socked her in the face—she was that close.

"They do an excellent pudding here."

She stared at the cups and container, clearly trying to figure out what I was doing. Even though I didn't get very far with martial arts when I was a kid, I remembered something my dad used to tell me: whoever throws the first punch is likely to win the fight. I couldn't underestimate Dana, and as horrible as she was, she wasn't stupid. She probably suspected why I was here as soon as she saw the food and tea. But she didn't know exactly what I'd bought, although she could probably go and delve into the mind of the guy who'd sold these to me. Nevertheless, I wasn't about to let her take my spoils away. I whispered the spell to send them home to my room.

The food and tea disappeared from my hands. Dana narrowed her eyes at me, then started laughing. "How refreshing. You're not as stupid as you look. Well, you probably are, but today you've had a burst of brain activity."

I would have liked to ask her why she was following me, but I didn't want to give her the satisfaction, and since I didn't want to hear anything else she had to say, I moved to the side in order to step around her. She grabbed my wrist and pushed me into the wall. If I wanted to go anywhere, I'd have to make a scene.

"You were told to stay away from PIB things, were you not?"

Her gaze was colder than an Alaskan winter, devoid of compassion or light. I hated showing weakness, but my body betrayed me by shivering. I managed to keep my voice nonchalant. "I was told never to go there. And I'm not there, so what's the problem?"

"You're meddling in matters that don't concern you. Investigate anything else, and I'll see to it that you're homeless. If you don't believe me, just think back to this morning. Who came to your defence? Oh, that's right, no one. And if losing your home isn't enough, Millicent only got a taste of what I'm capable of. Next time, the baby won't be so lucky." She cackled like the witch she was.

I shook my head slowly. What a freaking nutcase. She was the psychopathiest of psychopaths.

"You'll do well to fear me, petal. I'm going to leave you with a small reminder before we part ways. And if I catch you investigating so much as a drop of water…" My wrist stung where she gripped it, the pain building until it felt as if my whole arm was on fire. I whimpered. Tears came unbidden as I attempted to tear my arm out of her grasp.

My brain did its best to think through the pain, figure out how to get away, but it wouldn't work. Sweat dampened my forehead. Dizziness swept through my head. I swayed and fell back against the cool wall. I couldn't take much more. Not fighting back wasn't working. I needed to do something.

I focussed on my free arm that hung limply at my side. I could do this. I had to. Pretending to be defeated, I shut my eyes. Then I shot my elbow up and slammed it into her cheek. She grunted and stumbled back, releasing my wrist.

Thanks be to the gods; I was free. I ran for the toilets while whispering a return-to-sender spell. Once I reached the hand-washing area, I made my doorway and stepped through.

Finally in Angelica's reception room, I forced my breathing to slow as I looked at my wrist. The burn had faded to a sting, and the skin was fire-engine red, which looked great as nail polish, but as a skin tone, I'd had better. It was a miracle it wasn't blistered and burnt, considering the excruciating pain I'd experienced. I'd known she was spiteful and powerful, but I'd underestimated her lack of empathy and her willingness to physically harm me. I had no doubt now that she would kill Millicent's baby if she perceived me stepping out of line again. And unfortunately, I had a feeling she wouldn't stop there.

But neither would I. Letting her have free rein in the world was a horrendous idea. Come to think of it, what was her end game? Surely ruining my life wasn't the only thing she had on her to-do list.

I'd just have to figure out how to protect everyone I loved, fix Westerham's mess, and get rid of Dana before she ended up running the PIB. And I had to do it with limited support. At least Olivia and James were still on my side. I just hoped it stayed that way because I had a feeling we were going to be in for the fight of our lives—well, mine at least.

Except the fight for my life started earlier than I expected when I unlocked the reception-room door and stepped into the hallway.

Crap.

CHAPTER 6

I stepped into the hall. "Hi, L—" I just had time to fling my arm up in self-defence as Olivia swung a frying pan towards my head. It hit my forearm, and I screamed. Breath-stealing pain shot through my arm. She pulled her arm back over her head again, readying for another blow. Her eyes had the vacant manic stare of the other day. As her arm came down, I tucked my chin to my chest and leaped at her, catching her around her waist.

She slammed into the ground, and I landed on her. The momentum sent the pan flying into the wall behind us. She shrieked something unintelligible and grabbed my ponytail, yanking my head back. I wanted to repeat my spell from the other day, but she wasn't banging on my door so I couldn't use the same one. Trying to come up with a new one was hard while your hair was being ripped from your scalp.

I braced myself. "My friend Olivia is ripping my hair from my head. Put her to sleep until tomorrow afternoon, and transport her to her bed."

She disappeared from beneath me. I dropped to the floor with a thud and grunted. I turned my head so my cheek lay against the cool timber boards. Gross, I knew—because what if someone had dog-poo germs on their shoes and had walked here?—but it was as if someone had sucked all my energy out of my body. I yawned and contemplated staying there for a while. I'd definitely been doing too much magic today.

I was about to get settled in for the afternoon, but my arm wouldn't stop aching. I sighed, sending a small dust bunny tumbling across the floor. I imagined two mice with cowboy hats, one wearing a sheriff's badge, watching it roll by in a miniature Wild West.

I shook my head to clear it and sat up, my breath coming faster. I inspected my left forearm—the same one Witchface had burned or whatever she'd done. Red skin on my wrist: check. Egg-shaped bump on my forearm: check. Purpling commenced: check. My poor arm. What had it ever done to anybody?

I held my breath and listened. At least no noise came from upstairs, but just to be safe, I needed to check. I slowly stood, like the unfurling of a crinkled food wrapper, and then tiptoed up the stairs, careful to avoid the one tread on the first floor that always creaked. I silently made it to the second floor.

Her door was closed. Placing my ear to the timber, I strained to hear anything. Silence. My heart rate kicked up as I reached for the handle. *Please be asleep.* The handle turned without squeaking, thanks be to the gods. Opening it just enough to see in, I put my face to the small gap. She was on her back and fast asleep, snoring again. What the hell had set her off? She wouldn't have had time to go out and grab anything while I was gone. Was this residual magic from the original "poisoning"? I'd have to ask her when she woke. I quietly closed the door and went to my own room, locking the door behind me.

It was only once I was sitting on my bed, my back resting against the wall, that I let some of my stress out with a huff. What a crappy day. I didn't dare ask how it could be any worse. In fact, I was not looking forward to Angelica coming home. Would she act like she hated me, or would stupid Agent Laaam's influence only work while she was near her victims? Best not to assume anything where she was concerned. I'd wait here and pretend I was asleep until James contacted me. With the exception of going to the toilet, I was not going to leave this room.

I blinked. Oh my God! How had I forgotten? Sitting on my bedside table were the two cups of tea and pudding from the hospital. Then I realised why I was so tired. Not only had I put Olivia to sleep and relocated her upstairs, when I'd been in the hospital, I'd held a return-to-sender spell and travelled at the same time. I was actually witching rather well. Maybe I could really beat Dana. As much as I'd taunted her about my special talents, deep down, I recognised how much stronger a witch she was than me. But I was improving. There was hope for Westerham yet.

Although, when I slid forward to get off my bed and take a closer look at the food and drinks, my limbs shook. I was like a massive lump of jelly. My body did not want to cooperate. Maybe I should get some rest?

I pulled my phone out of my back pocket—how it had survived the past hour unscathed, I had no idea—and set the alarm to go off in two hours. Resting my head on the pillow, I did my best to ignore the throb in my arm. Thankfully, I was soon fast asleep.

⚜

MY EYES OPENED TO THE NON-MUSICAL REFRAIN OF THE "Strum" sound on my iPhone. Argh. I grabbed the phone and managed to turn the alarm off with clumsy fingers. Two hours' sleep was not enough, but I had work to do.

"Ah, bummer," I mumbled. I'd left the grimoire downstairs when I'd travelled to the hospital. I didn't want to waste my energy on magicking it up here, but neither did I want to run into Angelica if she were home. I settled for magic. It popped into existence on my bed next to me. I sat up and leant against my headboard, then settled the weighty tome on my lap.

So, what exactly did I need to do? I supposed looking for a magic signature would be first up, but if the magic had been cast on the ingredients before they went into the tea, it probably wouldn't show up, and I had no idea how magic reacted to things like boiling water. I knew magic signatures faded to nothing over time too, and we had no idea how long the perpetrator had waited between spelling the ingredients and getting them into circulation.

Paging through the grimoire, I finally found a detect-magic-signature spell. I snorted. I hadn't noticed before, probably because there was so much information in small lettering on each page, but every spell came with a ratings system like a recipe. There were four symbols in all. A little witch, complete with pointy witch's hat, a pointy hat by itself, a brain, and an exclamation mark in a triangle. Each picture was filled to varying degrees by black, although the exclamation mark one had red filling. For this spell, the witch only had her feet coloured in. The hat was a fifth coloured in, the brain a third, and the exclamation mark had a thin sliver of scarlet along the bottom. Why had I used that word: sliver? I hated that word. It was one of my most disliked words. Why did my brain hate me so much? It could have chosen any other word.

I flicked to the front of the book to see the key for the symbols. Hmm. The witch indicated how much energy the spell took to do—the fuller the witch, the more energy expended. The hat signified how much magic or power one had to draw. The brain was spell difficulty, and the exclamation mark in the triangle denoted potential to go wrong. I suspected that symbol was Angelica's favourite, and the redder, the better.

At least this was a relatively safe spell. The difficulty had me worried, though. Well, it wouldn't hurt to try—it might put me to sleep for a while, but whatever. I read through the instructions three times, then shut my eyes and went through it again, bit by bit, to make sure I understood what I had to do. It was rather tricky, so I read through it yet again. If Angelica wasn't tied up with stupid Piranha, I could have asked her to do this, but I couldn't trust her. I frowned, letting the sadness resettle like sand after disturbing the seafloor.

I took the lids off the tea, and I opened the pudding container. Mmm, that smelled good—the pudding that is. Maybe I should grab a coffee to go with it for when I finished? I was definitely on a roll with the brilliant ideas.

I started with the pudding. Chances were, the tea was the culprit, and I needed practice. I shut my eyes and imagined the river of power. I dipped into it with my imaginary hand, then pictured it forming a piece of white paper, which I could stick any symbols to, so I didn't have to memorise them. The image floated in my mind, first as a golden sheet, which then faded to white. I took a deep breath in and out. The first part was done. Now I had to hold that image in my mind while I did the next bit.

Keeping part of my thoughts on the paper, I drew more power from the never-ending source and formed a magical magnifying glass in the air with golden threads of magic. It was an outline, like the door. There was a more detailed spell where you could form the magnifying glass with your third eye, but I didn't have the skill for that. "A golden magnifying glass is what I need, to find the magical signatures I seek. Solidify now." I let more magic through in a trickle—if I fed too much through at once, it would shatter the delicate construct. As the image took on a three-dimensional quality, I reached out and gently grabbed the handle. "Well, holy cow. I did it!"

The handle was smooth, warm, and there was an almost imperceptible vibration to it, as if it were a living, breathing being. I could only guess at why. Maybe because the magic was alive?

Excitement spun and danced through me like an out-of-control dust devil, and I smiled. I was actually doing this. Now to see if it had really worked. I held the magnifying glass above the pudding, directed energy to my third eye, and looked at the food. If there were any magical signatures or traces of magic, it should show up.

I deflated, and my shoulders sagged. Nothing. Just pudding. I never thought I'd be disappointed at seeing *just pudding*. Either my magical item didn't work, or the food was fine. Maybe the tea would give me results I could be delighted with.

Saving my best bet for last, I hovered the magnifying glass over the English Breakfast. Nothing. Was I doing this right? I cricked my neck from side to side. Time for the final cup. I was going to be so disappointed if it came back blank, and I wouldn't know if I'd done the spell properly or if it was because the tea and pudding had never been tampered with. I guessed I could save it and show James.

I made a weird noise by vibrating my tongue on the roof of my mouth in an embarrassingly poor imitation of a drum roll. "Presenting… the last cup of tea. A hush falls over the crowd. Can Lily do it? Can she see the magic?" Yep, I was having fun with it. If I failed, at least I'd amused myself for a minute. And yeah, maybe I was stalling just a tad.

Time to pull up my big-girl pants and do this. One of Mum's favourite proverbs was, "Failure is a stepping stone to success." I clung to that sentiment as I placed the magnifying glass over the Earl Grey.

Oh my God. Was that magic? Small golden flecks, like glitter, floated in the tea. Some were on the top, but many were within the liquid and all the way to the bottom, if I wasn't mistaken. I magicked a glass from downstairs and poured half the tea into it, and yep, the flecks of gold were all through it. I was just about to stop watching and figure out what to do next, when a couple of the little flecks started flashing on and off. Weird. Okay, so weird was a relative term when observing magic golden bits in a cup of tea. After about thirty seconds of winking in and out, they disappeared.

Was the magic wearing out? Interesting. That meant I'd need to get this to James ASAP or get James to go order some for himself. But it wasn't safe to call or message him. I had to assume Dana had some way of spying on me or even both of us. I'd have to trust James knew what he was doing way more than I did and go with the flow. Gah,

Or maybe I didn't.

Maybe Dana had bugged our phones or houses magically or with normal technology, but surely she couldn't tell if I magicked something to James. But what if Millicent was under her spell and she figured out I'd sent the tea to James? She hadn't stood up for me the other day, although she had more important things to worry about. But before she'd been in pain, she had sat there mute like everyone else. I sighed. It was a sad day when you couldn't even trust your sister-in-law.

Hmm. There had to be a way to get a message to James. I was a witch, for goodness' sake. There must be something I could do that Dana couldn't police. My eyes widened. Could I send a written paper message to his pocket? That would be perfect.

I flicked back to the contents pages of the grimoire, my heart beating a bit faster. If it were possible, it would make such a difference. I slid my finger down the "s" page. Ah, here: *Sending Messages.* There were subsections: *voice messages*; *holographic messages*; *written messages*; *mind-to-mind messages*. Some of those were broken down into things like, if you wanted to leave a message in an inanimate object to be found at a later date, or if you wanted the message to appear immediately. The inanimate one would be something Angelica had told me about—agents could leave a message in a painting. When the agent receiving the message turned up, the painting would talk to them as if it were real.

I turned to page 2,254. Cripes, this book was huge, which was obvious by how much it weighed, but that huge? Maybe it was like the Tardis; it contained way more than what you thought. There was no way one book could have so many pages. Maybe the pages came into being based on what you were looking for? Argh! My brain was going off on too many tangents. I needed to stick to one thing at a time.

There it was. It was a fairly simple spell—similar to moving things from one room to another, or calling something to you when you wanted it; however, if you wanted to send something to someone else directly, you had to know their magic signature so the message could attach itself to that, unless you could see the person in real life, as in, they were in the same room. And the little icon that showed how much power was involved had three witches next to each other and three hats next to each other. The first witch and hat contained a thin strip of black filled in at the bottom. The middle witch and hat were a third filled, and the last witch and hat were full. A note underneath said: *This spell requires varying degrees of energy and power, which is distinctly correlated to the size and weight of the object being translocated and the distance involved.*

Okay. That part was fine, since the thing I wanted to translocate weighed practically nothing, and whilst James wasn't always in the UK, he didn't cross oceans—that I knew about. The problem was the magic signature. I had no idea what his was. Bummer.

Looked as if I was stuck here for the rest of the afternoon and night with nothing to do. I yawned, then realised I'd been holding onto the stream of power the whole time. I released it. The magnifying glass disappeared. I pouted.

"Bye, bye, magic construct. I'll miss you. You were my first, and I'll never forget you."

Well, if I wanted to make the most of my time, I'd just have to memorise some more spells. I sat back on my bed, grimoire on my lap, and studied as if my life depended on it.

Because I was pretty sure it did.

CHAPTER 7

The next morning, I woke to a new text message from James's burner phone. I lay on my back and held my phone in front of my face to read it. *Meet me at the gallery in front of the painting where you last saw your parents. Go there at 10:00 a.m. Leave your phone at home. Tell no one and delete this message straight away.*

He must fear my phone was bugged. I deleted the message and put my phone on my bed. It was nine thirty. I threw on a white T-shirt, black shorts, black cardigan, and sneakers—I wanted to be prepared in case there was any running in my near future. With everything that had been going on, it was always a possibility. At least I knew where we were going.

I had time, so I went next door and checked on Olivia. She was still sound asleep. Thank God. I then snuck downstairs—just in case Angelica was asleep, although that was unlikely, as she was an early riser— and magicked a cup of coffee. I had my coffee and a banana without any surprise visits. Then it was time to go. I hurried up to my room. After putting the lid back on the takeaway cup of Earl Grey, I grabbed it. This might be the only chance I had to show James.

I brought up my mind map and homed in on the National Gallery. I took a mental picture of the coordinates, made my door, and stuck them on the front.

I stepped through and into a clean cubicle. A toilet flushed in the stall next to mine. Wow, people must run through the front doors and straight to the toilet, which made sense if you'd travelled a long way to get here. I could imagine a bus full of elderly tourists would be totally busting by the time they got here from an hour or two away.

I waited for the person to wash and dry their hands. Except there was no washing or drying. Their cubicle door opened and closed, and then the main door to the bathroom clicked shut. Ew. I screwed up my face. Wash your hands, people! How gross. Now that person was distributing wee germs everywhere. I grabbed some toilet paper off the roll. I was not touching the door handle after that.

On my way to the Canaletto where I'd taken that picture of my parents, I dropped the toilet paper into the bin.

A seesaw of nerves played in my stomach. Up, down, up, down. This was the first time I'd been back since seeing my missing parents through my camera a couple of months ago. My talent had manifested through my Nikon, and I could see things that had happened in the past, as well as real-time people who would potentially die. I hadn't seen my parents since I was fourteen, and seeing them standing there had thrown me big time.

I swallowed as I stepped into the cavernous room that held such painful memories.

And there it was, one of Canaletto's magnificent Venetian landscapes, although that was a misnomer since there was a lot of water in the picture. James stood there, his back to me. I walked up and stood next to him, not sure what to expect. "Hey." My shoulders tensed. Was he still the James who loved me and would do anything to help me?

He looked down at me and put his arm around my shoulders, pulling me into a hug, which I gladly returned. "I'm so sorry, Lily. I could see what was happening in that meeting, but I didn't dare act. I need Dana to think she has me under control too." He dropped his arms, and I followed.

I gave him a small smile—it was a massive relief to know he could see through her crap. "It's okay. I understand, but at first... well, I thought everyone was under her spell. How come she can't influence us with her magic?"

"I'm not entirely sure, but it obviously has something to do with genetics and talents. Witches normally think of talents as stuff you can do. We don't consider them in terms of what others can't do to us, and to be honest, I've never met anyone who couldn't be swayed by an influencing spell. A couple of witches have tried it on me over the last few years, but I sensed it and blocked them. But being able to deflect it without trying—that's new."

"But I didn't feel any magic at the meeting. And I know that talents can be done 'silently,' but if she's compelling so many people at once, you'd expect to feel some kind of magic. How's she doing it?"

He frowned. "I don't know. It's possible she has some kind of cloaking device, but they're rare and illegal. If you channel your magic through one, it's undetectable by other witches, kind of like a silencer on a gun makes the shot quiet. If you were looking at her with your third eye, though, you'd likely see she was drawing magic. You just wouldn't know what for."

"I still can't believe she's duped Angelica."

"Angelica is fallible. She's one of the strongest witches I know, but Dana is too, and putting thoughts in people's heads in order to control them is her talent."

"And my phone?"

"Check it when you get home. Look at it with your third eye, and use a detect-magic spell. But don't do anything else. If you destroy the spell, she'll know. We need her to think we have no idea."

"Okay. Do you think she knows you still have your own mind?"

"No. Let's keep it that way."

"Okay. Also, I found magic in this tea. It's the one from

the hospital that Olivia drank before she went berserk the other day." I handed it to him.

He stared at me and blinked, obviously surprised. Why did everyone underestimate me all the time? He took the lid off and looked inside. The warm tingle of someone using magic caressed the back of my neck. At least it didn't feel icky, like Dana's had.

"Brilliant, Lily! Great work." He looked at me and smiled. Then his smile fell, and he shook his head. "The PIB hasn't tested anything from anywhere yet, other than the blood tests they conducted on the victims. They're busy compiling information before they do anything else."

"Let me guess. Dana's in charge of that part of it?"

"No, actually, Angelica is, but Dana's controlling her now, as you know."

"Why do you think she's hindering things?"

He shrugged one shoulder. "Only two reasons I can see. One is that she wants Angelica and Drake to fail, paving the way for her to get a promotion. The other answer is one I like even less. She has a hand in the strife going on in Westerham."

"That crossed my mind too. But what would she get out of it, other than the promotion thing? Maybe the two are related?" It would actually be easier if she was the one messing everything up—one perpetrator would be easier to catch than two or more. Knowing our luck, she wasn't behind it all."

"Maybe? But honestly, Lily, I don't really believe she has

a hand in what's going on out there. She's never made a secret of the fact that she wants to run the PIB one day. This could be her ticket. I know the nameless, faceless bosses who call the shots from above have had Drake on probation for the last three months. That thing with his niece put him on their radar."

He'd given his niece, Snezana, a job at the PIB. She was the reason I'd found myself over here in the first place. She'd kidnapped James, and then she tried to kill me. Will ended up shooting her to save me. He'd killed her, but even though she was gone, the repercussions of her actions were still being played out.

"Whatever her reasons, how do we defeat her? She found me at the hospital yesterday after I'd gotten the samples. She burnt my wrist and told me if I kept investigating, she'd kill your baby. She was the one who gave Millicent those cramps the other day. Dana had threatened me earlier. That was just a warning. Next time, she plans to follow through."

His face paled. I put a reassuring hand on his forearm. His gaze met mine, blazing with fury so hot that I could imagine his eyelashes melting. His voice was low, urgent. "How do you know she gave Millicent those cramps?"

"She said if I stepped out of line, she was going to hurt those I loved in ways I can't imagine. That's pretty much a direct quote. She said that to me the day I was in there answering phone calls. And at the meeting, just after Millicent started having the cramps, Dana told me if Millicent loses her baby, it would be all my fault. Don't you remember?"

"No, sorry. I was preoccupied with other things." He stared past my shoulder, likely thinking. His jaw muscles bunched, and I could hear what sounded like his teeth grinding against each other. Yikes.

"Please tell me you have a plan to stop her. If we don't, she'll be running the PIB in no time. Plus, she wants me dead. I'm practically a prisoner in my own home. If she sees me anywhere, she can pretend she thinks I'm investigating, even if I'm not. Plus, the baby." I bit my lip and waited.

He finally looked at me. "You bet we're going to take her down. No one gets away with harming my wife, my sister, and especially not my unborn child. I'm afraid we can't trust Millicent right now. I'm pretty sure she would side with Dana at the moment, but I can't mess with anything. We need Dana to think she has me in her pocket too."

I'd suspected as much, but I was still sad that Millicent wasn't herself. "Oh, I almost forgot. Can you give me your magic signature? I can send you notes if I have it. Then we don't have to send text messages. Maybe we could even send some fake text messages that backup what we want her to think."

He raised his brows. "You've really come a long way, Lily. That's a brilliant idea! Where did you get that spell from?"

"The grimoire Will lent me. I have it at home. I've been practicing, hence the cup." I nodded towards the tea he still held. "At least we have somewhere to start. I have a feeling it's in all sorts of tea, although it wasn't in the English Breakfast her dad had at the same time. And think about it; what better way to poison lots of English people than to put something in their national beverage?"

"Now we have to narrow down where it's coming from. Once we do that, we can grab a magic signature. Great work, Lil." He smiled.

Warmth spread through my stomach. I was proud of myself, but knowing James was proud made it that much sweeter. "So, now what? Is there anything I can do?"

He pressed his lips together, then said, "Lay low for now. I'll see what I can come up with without Dana figuring it out. I could gather samples for the PIB. I'll check it all out before they get it, though. When I have a breakthrough, I'll let you know. But once we figure the who and how, we'll need to have a plan to bring Dana down. If we give her any chance to benefit from this, it will be that much harder to get rid of her."

Argh, lay low. That meant I was stuck inside. I supposed I could still go for my morning jogs, although there could be someone new looking for me now that the two thugs who were after me were dead. We still hadn't figured out who was ultimately behind the kidnap and killing attempts. Oh no! "If Dana knows Millicent is pregnant, could that group who are after me know?"

He blew out a loud breath and ran a hand through his dark hair. "Damn. You're right. I don't know how she knows. We haven't told anyone, and Mill's not really showing. So now Drake knows and those two agents who were in the meeting. Shit."

"Mill rubs her tummy sometimes without realising it. It's a dead giveaway. That's probably how Dana worked it out." I sighed. It seemed the baby bump was well and truly out of the bag. "So, can I grab your signature?"

"Okay." He held my hands. "I'm going to send it to you, like Angelica did in Paris, with the coordinates."

Oh, hang on. I took down my mind shield. "Cool. I'm ready." I shut my eyes so I could better concentrate. James's intricate golden signature appeared in my mind. It was all loopy squiggles on the outside, becoming denser as it moved into the middle so that in the centre, it looked as if a three-year-old had attacked a piece of paper with lots of energy and no finesse. I took a mental photograph of it and opened my eyes. "Thanks." I redid my thought-protection bubble. It had finally become a habit. I hadn't had any mortifying mind-reading incidents for weeks.

James looked into my eyes. "It's time to go. I have to get back to an investigation. If I'm gone much longer, word might get back to Dana. She hasn't got control of everyone, but I'm sure she's got enough eyes and ears out there. It would be the normal thing for anyone wanting to take over. I'll let you know when I have news. But stay safe. Okay? And don't forget: I love you. I will never side with anyone against you." He enveloped me in a hug.

"Thanks. You be careful too." I blinked back tears. To know my brother still loved me meant everything.

He pulled away, and we walked to the toilets.

As I stepped into the cubicle, I wondered how long it would be till I saw him again. I knew there was going to be a lot of angst between now and then. I just hoped when everything was over, it went our way, because if it didn't, the world was going to be a much crappier place.

I would just have to make sure we won. Or die trying.

CHAPTER 8

Later in the afternoon, while I was reading a book on my iPad—I figured I needed some time out, and I felt safest in my locked bedroom—a knock sounded on my door. Olivia's tentative voice said, "Lily, are you in there?" She sounded normal, thank God.

I got up and stood next to the door. "Is that *normal* Olivia asking or psycho Olivia?"

"Normal, apologetic, bad-friend Olivia. I'm so sorry, Lily. Can I come in?"

I opened the door to her sad face.

"Hey. What happened?" The right thing to do to make her feel better would be to give her a hug, but the part of my brain that was into self-preservation made me stand back.

"After you left, Angelica came home."

Oh, crap. If she'd known I was out, she would have told Dana.

What I was thinking must have been on my face because Olivia gently placed her hand on my arm. "It's okay. I told Angelica you were asleep, that you didn't feel well after what happened at the meeting."

"Oh my God. Thank you!" This time I ignored my brain and hugged her. "Why don't we continue this conversation in your room?" I wanted to stay away from my phone, but I'd explain that to her when we were out of earshot of my electronics.

"Okay, sure." She led the way into her bedroom and sat on her bed.

I looked around her room. I found what I wanted on her desk. I picked up her phone and put my finger against my lips in a shushing gesture. She nodded. I ducked back to my room and left her phone there before returning and shutting her door. I made a bubble of silence, then sat next to her. I sighed. "Okay, we're secure. We can talk."

"What was that about?"

"I'm pretty sure Dana's listening in. At the very least, she's bugged my phone so she can track where I am. While you were asleep"—I smiled sheepishly. Yes, I'd put her to sleep for a good reason, but still, it was weird—"I met up with James."

"Oh my goodness. That's awesome! What did he say?"

"He definitely hasn't been taken over by Dana. He was going along with everything so he could work out what was going on. We can't trust Millicent, though."

Her face fell. "Oh. That's terrible."

I nodded. "Anyway, he told me to check my phone for tampering. When I came home and looked at my phone with my third eye, I found a symbol, which I magicked onto a piece of paper and sent to James. He confirmed it's a spying bug. As well as tracking me, she can listen to my conversations if the phone is within hearing distance. She may have bugged your phone somehow too. Although, since you've never met her, it's less likely. I don't think you can put magic on something you can't see."

"Yes, but what if she got Angelica to do something to my phone?"

Crap. She made a good point. "It's possible." Argh, could this day get any more depressing? I should not be asking that question and tempting fate. "I'll test your phone later, but we can't unbug it because she'll know. We'll just go along with it and feed her fake information."

Olivia grinned. "Ooh, I like the sound of that."

I smiled. Giving her the runaround could be fun, but then I remembered she'd take any aggravation out on those I cared about. *Repeat after me, Lily. I should not poke the piranha. I should not poke the piranha.* "So… what happened yesterday? Was it something you ate or drank, or did you just get angry all of a sudden?"

She blushed. "Ah… I really am sorry. I wonder if I should just be locked up for a week or something, make sure I'm really over it."

"I know you're sorry, Liv. It wasn't even your fault. If we

want to stop it from happening again, I need to know how it happened."

"I didn't go anywhere, I swear. I wasn't even going to have anything. After you left, I went and turned on the TV downstairs. About five minutes later, Angelica came home with two cups of tea—one for her, one for me—and a coffee for you. She said she wanted to apologise for what happened in the meeting."

Colour me sceptical, but I bet Angelica hadn't come up with the idea herself. This was worrying, though. It meant we weren't safe, even at home. Dana had a minion who lived on the inside to do her bidding. Crap. "And you drank the tea?"

"Yes, obviously."

"Where's the cup?"

"In the bin in the kitchen."

I jumped up and hurried down the stairs, taking them two at a time. In the kitchen, I went straight to the cupboard under the sink, where we had a small bin we emptied every day or two.

Empty. Damn!

The next stop was the big bin outside—the one the council emptied each week.

It sat to the right of the front door, about five metres away, behind a hedge—it wouldn't do to have visitors seeing the garbage bin. It came up to just below my chest, so if it were only half full, I was going to have to lean into it. I swallowed before flipping the lid open.

My heavy sigh contained as much drama as I could muster. The bin was only half full. I fake cried.

"What's wrong?" Olivia had found me and joined me at the bin.

"I'm going to have to go through the bin. Gross."

"This is all my fault. I'll do it." She moved to get past me to the bin opening.

"No! It's not your fault. This is all stupid Witchface. I'm not holding anyone else accountable. Angelica is going to flip when she finds out what happened. I would not want to be Witchface then, but I do want to watch." I smirked. Oh, the things Angelica would do. The crap was totally going to hit the fan, and I couldn't wait. Realising this gave me extra incentive to go through the bin. I conjured the rubber gloves from the laundry, and they appeared on my hands.

"Nice trick." Olivia smiled. "I wish I was a, *you know*. Can you become one, or do you have to be born into it?"

"You have to be born into it, but trust me, it's not all that great. My life has pretty much gone to hell because of it. I'd much rather I was back in Sydney in ignorance of it. The only good thing to come of me being here is meeting you, seeing my brother and Millicent, and getting to know Angelica, Beren, and Sarah."

She grinned. "I think you left someone out."

"Oh, did I? Whoever could that be?" I rolled my eyes. "Oh, look. I have garbage to go through." I turned and held my breath while I peered in. Surely it would be on the top since it would have been in the last lot of rubbish to be tipped in there. "Is that it?" Thankfully, the two takeaway cups were only half buried. Fingers crossed one was hers.

She looked in. "Yes. That looks like them."

I stepped away from the rubbish, took a deep breath, and held it. I leaned in and snatched the two cups out. I'd be sad if neither of them was the right cup—Olivia had mentioned Angelica had also come bearing coffee.

"What kind of tea was it?"

"Mine was Earl Grey. I don't know what hers was."

I screwed up my face. I did not want to smell those cups, but it had to be done. "Okay. I'm going in." I lifted them to my nose, one at a time. They smelled like Earl Grey tea and rotting vegetables. I gagged. "I think they're both Earl Grey. Can you check?" Why should I have all the fun?

Olivia's expression left no doubt in my mind that this was about as appealing to her as realising you've stepped in dog poo. "Do you really need me to do this?"

"Yes. I'm pretty sure I know what Earl Grey smells like, but I could be wrong, and since you drink it all the time, it would be sensible for me to get your opinion. Plus, you should really know my pain." I smirked.

"Ha ha, very funny. But you're right." She stared at the cups for a moment before giving me the nod. I lifted them to her nose. She sniffed one, then the other, and turned her head. "Argh, gross. I think you may have ruined Earl Grey tea for me forever."

"So it is?"

"Yes."

"Thanks. You're awesome."

"I try." She smiled and shook her head.

We went back inside to the kitchen sink. I put the cups in there and magicked the grimoire down. After reading through the same spell as yesterday, I created my magnifying glass. I didn't bother with the imaginary paper, as there would be no symbol to find.

"Oh my God. Did you just make that out of magic?" Olivia's eyes were huge.

"Yes, I did. Cool, huh?"

"Way cool." She smiled.

There was pretty much nothing left in the cups, except the stench of decay, so it would be a miracle if I found traces of golden energy. If the magic had any kind of intelligence, it would not be hanging out in those cups. Nevertheless, I positioned my magnifying glass over the first cup. Were those little glittery things? I bent my face closer and squinted. It didn't really help to squint. Why did everyone think it did? It was actually worse as my eyelashes got in the way.

I slid my magical construct over the other cup. Yep, there were definitely traces of power. I'd love to bag them and send them to James, but someone would be sure to see them—they weren't just little pieces of paper I could send straight to his pocket. I released the stream of power, and my magnifying glass disappeared.

Olivia was watching me. "And?"

I contained us in a bubble of silence. "There are traces of magic in both. The spell doesn't work on witches, so Dana didn't bother making a special cup."

"Are you sure it was Dana and not an accident? What if it was Angelica?" Her brow wrinkled, and she bit her bottom lip.

My stomach dropped. To think Angelica would endanger our lives like that was too much to process. "Pretty sure. Angelica probably told her what had happened with you and me the other day, and she's decided since I'm stuck at home, to make my life as terrible as possible. And that's the first time Angelica has brought us hot beverages out of the blue. Also, if Angelica did think of it herself, we know someone else was behind her thoughts. I won't ever believe Angelica would hurt either of us intentionally."

"True. So, what now?"

"I'm going to throw these back in the bin. There's no point keeping them for evidence because the traces of magic will disappear soon, and I can't send them to James without blowing his cover. But at least we know. I'm sorry, but you're going to have to stop drinking tea until this is all over."

Her eyes widened, horror shining from their depths. "You can't ask me to do that. Can we just get some from somewhere else that doesn't have contaminated tea?"

"Ah, yes, we can." Why didn't I think of that? I really was stupid sometimes. "To be safe, maybe go to Scotland or something." I laughed, but I wasn't really joking.

"I was thinking more of London. The violence hasn't reached there yet. I'll catch the train because I've got study to do. I've lost a lot of time sleeping lately." She raised a brow and put her hands on her hips.

"Yeah, yeah, but would you rather have a dead friend?"

She sobered at that, and her hands dropped to her sides. "No. I'm sorry. This whole thing's been horrible."

"And it's worse standing here smelling garbage. I'm going to put these back." I took the cups and threw them away. Then I went inside, washed the gloves, and put them back under the sink. Olivia was making herself a cheese sandwich.

Something she'd said bothered me. That one word: yet. We didn't know who was truly behind these, for want of a better word, poisonings, so their motivation was a mystery. Dana may be part of it, but I highly doubted she was the only one involved. What if they were just getting started with Westerham? What if London would soon suffer the same fate? My stomach dropped as I envisioned the worst-case scenario. Utter disaster. What if Westerham was a test for rolling this out to the rest of the world? Obviously tea wouldn't reach as many people elsewhere, but coffee and all sorts of other popular drinks both hot and cold could be targeted.

I dropped into a dining chair. Olivia finished making her sandwich and sat opposite me. "What's wrong?"

"What if whoever's doing this doesn't stop at Westerham and Kent?"

The blood drained from her face. "Oh dear."

"Oh dear, indeed."

CHAPTER 9

That evening, as I was readying for bed and brushing my teeth in the main bathroom, Angelica appeared at the door. I froze and looked at her through the mirror. She was holding onto the doorframe, and her cheeks were flushed. She didn't look well. I hadn't been sure what to expect when I finally saw her, but this wasn't it. There were even a few tendrils of hair loose from her bun, and that never happened.

I turned around. "Are you all right?"

She looked at me, confused. "Lily?"

I wrinkled my forehead. Was she kidding? "Yes, it's me. Are you sick?"

"Yes. I don't feel well at all. I'm dizzy and have a headache. I may even have a temperature."

"Do you want help getting to your room?"

"Yes, I think so. Thank you."

I spat the toothpaste in the sink and rinsed my mouth. Then I helped her downstairs and to her room. She sat on the bed and placed a hand on her forehead.

I gazed around her spotless bedroom, wondering if I should offer to help her change. It was awkward. I wasn't used to seeing her like this, and I knew she wasn't used to asking for help. Had Dana's tampering with her mind injured her? Or had Dana put something in the tea that would affect her? I stopped staring out the window at her back garden and fields beyond. As embarrassed as she would probably be when she had her right mind back, she needed my help now. Feeling uncomfortable wasn't going to help.

"Do you need me to help you change for bed?"

"Ah, no. I think I can manage." Her normally strong voice was meek, uncertain.

"Where do you keep your pyjamas?"

"That drawer over there." She pointed to her built-in wardrobe. I opened the door she'd pointed at. "The second drawer from the top."

I opened it and pulled out a pair of short-sleeved blue ones with knee-length pants. I held them up for her to see. "Are these okay?"

"Yes, thank you, dear."

I handed them to her. She stared at me, her brow furrowed.

"Do you need anything else? Would you like me to call Beren?" I wasn't sure what the protocol was for ill witches. Would a normal doctor be fine, or did they need a witch doctor? And not the tribal kind. Beren was an exceptional healer, and he could probably help.

"I don't think so. A good night's rest is all I need. I haven't slept for two days." That'd do it. "So much work to do. I would have stayed at work, but Agent Lam sent me home. Dana is such a treasure. She'll be running the PIB one day. It will be wonderful to have a woman in charge."

I practiced my poker face, but in her state, she likely wouldn't notice my shock or disdain. Whatever Dana had done to her had really messed her up. I'd never seen her so, well, old and subservient. She was behaving like a ninety-year-old, not someone in their fifties. I mean, the Angelica I knew would never be sent home by anyone. The concept was almost unthinkable. And even though she'd never said she wanted a promotion, I'd always assumed she was next in line whenever Drake left. "Are you sure you're fine to get changed?"

"Yes, thank you."

"Okay, but if you need anything, let me know."

"Certainly, but I don't trust you, truth be told. I'd feel better if you left now."

Had someone just stabbed me in the heart with a knitting needle? Because it sure felt like it. I bit my tongue against the tears that wanted out. Not trusting myself to speak, I nodded and left, closing the door quietly behind me.

Anger sizzled through my body. I swear I heard it crackling in the air around me. Bloody Agent Lam. Why did she hate me so much? First she wanted me away from Will.

Then it was out of the PIB. Now she wanted everyone I cared about to hate me too. I must pose some kind of danger to her. Okay, so I wasn't hypnotisable. That made me a small threat, but since no one was listening to me, how was that going to harm her? Unless…

Unless I was way more powerful than I thought. She knew something I didn't. Ah, the irony. She wanted to know my secret, yet she knew a secret about me that I didn't. But what, and how? Had William told her about my ability to photograph past events? Maybe she knew about that, but she thought there was also a different secret?

Argh! I couldn't stand in the corridor all night and guess, because one thing was for sure. Time was becoming critical. She'd effectively just gotten rid of Angelica, and I'd bet that whatever she'd done to her was going to last more than another day. If she was going to make a move for the top job, it was going to happen soon. Not that I cared what happened at the PIB, except that if she was running things, the whole of the UK was in trouble. She'd be more likely to collude with the criminals than put them away. Would she put me in jail on trumped-up charges?

Too many questions, and no answers. It was time to consult the grimoire. Maybe there was at least one answer in there. If I could find out what was wrong with Angelica, I could help her, and I could avoid calling Beren, who would report back to Witchface.

Right. I was going to figure this out one problem at a time, and when I had all the answers, she'd better watch out.

Tyrants had no place in this world, and I'd get rid of her if it was the last thing I did.

I stayed up reading until 3:00 a.m. I finally had to stop because I couldn't see properly through my watering eyes, care of all the yawning. After such a mammoth effort, I slept until ten. When I got up, I dressed, then went down to Angelica's room to see if she was okay. Her distrust of me wasn't enough to keep me away. I really had no idea what Witchface had done to her and how sick she might get.

I knocked on her door but received no answer. I rapped a second time, but still nothing. Was she even in there? She could have felt better and gone to work.

I opened the door and peered in. She was in bed, asleep. "Angelica?" My voice was quiet, timid. It felt weird being in her bedroom while she was asleep, and I hated waking people. Also, I didn't want to frighten her. Even if she recognised me, she was sure to be surprised at seeing someone in her room, and she might zap me with a spell.

But I needn't have worried—she didn't stir. I forced myself to speak in a normal voice. "Angelica, are you okay?" Her silence didn't bode well. I slowly moved three steps forward. "Hello, it's me." Her eyes remained closed. A dog barked next door, and I jumped, my heart hammering. I placed my hand on my chest and shook my head. *Idiot, Lily. She's not dead. She's just asleep.* If that was the truth, why wasn't she moving?

I stared at the sheet covering her chest and stomach, straining to see the telltale movement, however small, that would indicate she was breathing. I bit my lip and forced myself to close the remaining distance to her bedside. I was sure I saw the tiniest lift, then fall. To be sure, I placed my palm in front of her mouth. Thank God. She was alive. Talk about overreacting. Of course she was alive, but why wasn't she waking up?

I placed my hand on her forehead. It was hot, way hotter than it should be, and she didn't so much as turn her head or open her eyes at my touch. Stuff Witchface; I needed to call Beren.

I travelled my phone to my hand and dialled. Would he even answer it, knowing it was me?

Nope. It went to message bank. "Hi. You've reached Beren DuPree. Please leave a message." *Beep.*

"Hi, Beren, it's me, the most-hated witch ever. I'm calling because Angelica is sick… very sick, and she needs your help. She's at her house in bed with a terrible fever, and she won't wake up. Please help." *Beep.* Wow, that was only just enough time to say everything I needed to. He may not want to answer my call, but hopefully, he would come when he realised what the problem was. Unless…. What if Dana had put the idea into everyone's head that Angelica being sick wasn't an issue and that she'd get better without intervention?

"Argh!" This was beyond frustrating. Did James know much about healing? I grabbed my notebook and wrote to him. *Angelica is really sick. Tried calling Beren. Got no response. Can you help?* I sent the note with the spell I learned two days ago, directly to James's pocket.

About five minutes later, a note appeared in my shorts

pocket. *I might be able to help, but I'm in the middle of something that I can't leave. I'll drop by tonight.*

Damn. There was no one else I could ask.

My phone dinged with a message, and I started. Had Beren replied? I looked at the screen, which showed a number I didn't recognise.

Oh, how sweet. You're worried about Angelica. I'm sure she'll be fine. We all get sick sometimes. Beren won't be coming to help. He understands she's just exhausted and will return to work in a few days. How are Millicent and the baby doing, petal? Anyway, must toddle off. Tomorrow is going to bring exciting things. Very exciting. Toodles. She ended it with a crying-laughing emoji.

"Grrrr." I clenched my jaw and rubbed my arm where goosebumps had formed. Well, that proved she was spying on my phone, although I'd pretty much known she was. I just hadn't thought contacting Beren to help someone else was disallowed. And what would tomorrow bring? That was the part that really worried me.

I was supposed to stay in my room and not interfere in anything. Well, sorry, Witchface, but I didn't do well with being ordered around.

I left my phone on my bed and went and knocked on Olivia's door. No answer. I opened it and looked in. She was gone, probably on the train to London to get some tea. I was on my own.

Again.

If I was going to deal with this, I needed coffee. I went down to the kitchen and turned on the coffee machine Will had given me. It seemed like a lifetime ago but had only been a few months. I leaned back on the counter behind me and hugged myself. I missed him and his cranky self, dammit. The heated looks he used to give me were like nothing else I'd ever experienced, and when he smiled, I felt it all the way to my toes. Maybe she'd just gotten her hooks into him earlier than everyone else. He could have been her test subject—if she could get him to fawn over her again, taking control of everyone else would be a cinch.

And yes, I saw it could just be wishful thinking on my part, but what if it wasn't? And what would she do when she didn't need everyone because she got her promotion? My eyes widened. What if she kept them as her slaves forever?

Nausea wrapped firm hands around my throat and squeezed. I swallowed against it, but it didn't help. There had to be a way to defeat her.

The light on the machine came on, indicating it was ready to caffeinate. Oh, no. There were no beans left—the container was empty, and then I remembered I'd poured the last of them into the machine the other day. Crap. I was going to have to go out.

I'd leave my phone at home, but what if Dana found out? Her first target would be Millicent. Hmm, an idea was forming. I went back upstairs and grabbed my notebook and pen. *Need to go out and get coffee. If Dana finds out, she may hurt Millicent. I know me going out is against Dana's rules, but I think we're beyond that. And something big is happening tomorrow—she texted me. There's no point obeying the law if she isn't—we'll never win. Your talent is the same as Dana's. I know you don't have anything to help hide the magic, but you're married to Millicent. She trusts and loves you. Can you make her think she's in pain or doesn't feel well? Make her panic so you have to take her to the hospital or home? Just get her out of Dana's way. Also, if Dana thinks Millicent is having real problems, she won't bother with her. Let me know ASAP if you can do this. Maybe I can gather some other evidence while I'm out. I'll take my camera. We're running out of time.*

I magicked it to him and crossed my fingers. While I waited for his response, I checked on Angelica. She was still dead to the world, but not, ah, dead, dead, thank goodness. Her forehead still felt hot, although it was hard to tell whether it was actually hotter. I should take her temperature properly.

I turned and looked at the door to her en suite. Going in there and searching her drawers was a terrible invasion of privacy, but this was an extenuating circumstance. Normal, unaffected-by-Dana Angelica would probably be okay with me looking. If I couldn't find a thermometer, I'd pick one up while I was out.

As I stepped over the threshold of the en suite, Angelica groaned. I spun around. Her face was contorted in what I could only assume was pain. What the hell was I supposed to do? I had no idea how to check her out with magic. Did she have a normal doctor she called or even another witch-type doctor like Beren? She settled, but her forehead stayed creased, as if she were still in a bit of pain or worried. Her subconscious probably tried to tell her what was going on.

Should I search for another doctor's number? If she had one, it would probably be saved in her phone, and I didn't have access to that. Seriously, this was impossible. I turned back to the en suite, then towards Angelica, then the en suite again. Taking her temperature wasn't going to achieve much, although, if it were crazy high, I could call an ambulance. Fine. That was my plan, as pathetic as it was.

I opened one drawer after the other, until I'd searched all four of them. Then I opened the cupboard doors and went through everything under the vanity sink. Nothing. I dropped to my bottom on the cold tile floor and hung my head. I didn't do useless.

One bum cheek warmed slightly. Huh? Oh, it must be a message from James! I stood and reached into my back pocket. The joyous sensation of paper against my fingertips made me smile. I snatched it out and opened it.

Hi, Lily. You know I don't like breaking the law, but I'll admit, I don't have any other solutions. I'll take Millicent somewhere to eat for lunch, and I'll convince her she's not well, and she should go to her parents'. I've been doing some investigating of my own. I've checked out twelve of the places people had visited the day they turned violent. All of the shops or cafés get their tea supplies from the same place. I haven't dug any deeper yet because Drake has me on a different case. I've only tested samples from one of the places, and it had traces of magic, like the one you got from the cafeteria. I'm not sure at this point what you can help with, but maybe go and take some photos of W & W Tea Supplies. Their address is Block 4 Vestry Trading Estate Vestry Road, Sevenoaks J.

Okay, that could work. I magicked my notebook and pen to myself and wrote a note to confirm where I was going and that I was leaving my phone at home. After sending it to James, I checked Angelica as I went through her room—no change. I wanted to tell her I was going to help, that it would all be okay, but if Angelica somehow got better in the next hour and told Dana, I'd draw attention to myself.

I shut her door quietly as I left, not that the noise would bother her. I frowned. I'd only ever known her as capable, and quite scary, to be honest. Seeing her incapacitated unsettled me. It had taken me a while to adjust to my new witchy reality, and much of my world was built on the foundations of Angelica's strength and wisdom, her ability to keep things ordered and safe. But Dana was eroding that foundation faster than a tsunami.

I took a deep breath and went up to my room. I grabbed my knapsack and chucked in my notebook and pen, camera, wallet, cardigan, and umbrella—stupid English weather. It wasn't raining now, but who knew when it would decide to? It often rained on and off several times a day, even if the morning had started sunny. The English weather was reliably unreliable.

When I stepped outside and shut the front door, I shivered. The day was warm, maybe twenty-four or twenty-five degrees, but the risk I was taking by leaving the house was something I couldn't ignore. My gaze darted around. Was she watching somehow? If she was, she probably wouldn't think anything of me going to Costa, but later, when I jumped on the bus and went to W & W Tea Supplies, she'd realise. I had to cross my fingers, toes, arms, and anything else I could think of that she had no way of tracking me except my phone.

As I hurried up the lane, the sweet smell of freshly cut grass did its best to remind me of summer days when I was a kid, when Dad would mow the lawn, and James and I would run in front of him, pretending to be scared of the "monster" trying to eat us. Then, when the mowing was done, he'd turn the sprinkler on, and we'd run around under it for hours.

The heaviness of tears pulsed behind my eyes. I'd only just begun to rebuild a life with friends who had become family. There was no way in hell Dana was going to take it away.

My footfalls came with increased purpose as I strode up the slight rise towards the high street. At the top of the rise, I turned left. Cars whizzed past, but not as many as usual, and I could count the pedestrians on one hand. In fact, uniformed army personnel outnumbered civilians three to one. The recent violence had laid waste to the retail heart of Westerham and made it look like a war zone, minus the rubble and tanks. My mouth dropped open. Oh, hang on, there *was* a small tank blocking the side road next to the village green.

Who had done this, and why? Dana may want to solve this herself and take all the credit, but she was unlikely to be the perpetrator, even though she *could* do it. While I fumed about Dana and fighting her, the real perpetrator was free to get away with it until the PIB got its act together. Hopefully I could discover something this afternoon that would bring us closer to catching the person responsible. And wouldn't that be nice, if I could surprise Dana with the criminal and ruin her chances for a promotion. If James and I did manage to crack the case, I'd make sure the credit went to Angelica. How, I had no idea, but we'd think of a way.

Costa smelled as delicious as ever, but the happy chattering British accents that normally filled the place had given way to the low intermittent hum of only two tables of two people each. I had the pick of seats today and no queue. The teenager behind the register smiled at me. "What can I get for you?"

"I'd like a skim milk cappuccino and double-chocolate muffin, thanks." I hadn't treated myself to muffin decadence for at least a week, and I needed cheering up. I was not going to feel guilty for eating a week's worth of calories in one meal today.

I handed him exact change and stood to the side to await my order. I wondered if Olivia had found her tea yet and if London was still calm. I'd forgotten to check on the news this morning. But I had a feeling it would only be a matter of time before the violence spread to London and beyond.

A young woman placed my order on the bench. "Thanks." I grabbed it and took one of the vacant window seats. It was unheard of to have this much choice. There were days when it was so crowded—usually on the weekend when it was raining—that you had to get a takeaway order.

The first bite of muffin melted in my mouth, coating my tongue. "Mmmm." God, that was good. "Oh, how I've missed you, chocolatey yumminess. You too, cappuccino." I looked up. One of the other occupied tables happened to be two tables away from me, and one of the thirty-something-year-old women was staring at me, her expression mildly alarmed. I smiled and shrugged. I was getting acquainted with my brunch. Nothing weird about that.

She turned away and whispered something to her friend. I think I liked this place better when it was crowded. No one would have noticed my private conversation to my coffee and muffin with all that noise.

As I ate, army personnel wandered up and down the high street, occasionally stopping to debrief each other—okay, so they were probably just chatting, but they looked so official doing it. I giggled as I thought about how they'd be at home. Did their kids have to do lots of push-ups? "Tommy, I told you to tidy your room. Drop and give me twenty!" I would have been the push-up queen. I hadn't had a tidy room until becoming a witch and being able to zap stuff into the cupboard.

Soon enough, I'd finished, and it was time to figure out how to get to Sevenoaks. There was a bus that went, but I had no idea how close it would get me to my actual destination. Although I didn't mind a bit of a walk if it came to that. I went to the green and waited at the bus stop with my Connected Kent and Medway card out and ready. I didn't catch public transport often, but when I did, there was nothing worse than someone getting on the bus and taking five minutes to find their card. I mean, you know you're catching the bus. How hard was it to be prepared?

I read the bus timetable. My bus should be here within the next five minutes. Public transport in the UK was way better than Sydney's. We had to wait ages for buses and trains, and they didn't always go where you needed them to.

The bus arrived, and I hopped on. Again, it was easy to find a seat. It was good that most people were staying home, but it did feel eerie, almost post-apocalyptic. If this continued, businesses would shut down for good. You could last only so long without income. I slumped back into my seat and stared out the window. I hoped Westerham could go back to how it was soon, but how many relationships would be permanently damaged? We wouldn't know the true toll for weeks. Another incentive to shut this crap down ASAP.

The further we got from Westerham, the more people were about, although it wasn't a lot more. The contamination had affected all of Kent, from what I'd seen on the news.

It took around seventeen minutes to get to Sevenoaks Railway Station. I had to change buses. It only took a few minutes of travelling north to reach Bat and Ball Railway station, and from there I had to walk. I'd asked the bus driver how long the walk was—around twenty minutes. I was glad the weather had decided to be unpredictably predictable. Because I didn't have my phone, I pulled up the Westerham map in my mind, using the river of golden power. Being a witch made life so much easier. If only there were more public toilets set up around the place, I could have travelled there the easy way, but then I wouldn't get to act like a tourist and watch the countryside go by.

Sweat slicked my forehead, but finally, there it was, the sign for Vedry Road. Large warehouses lined it—both modern metal buildings and older brick ones. It wasn't the prettiest of areas. Cars were parked along the street, and there was very little vegetation. I would probably look a bit suspicious taking photos—it wasn't exactly a tourist destination. My phone would have been subtler, but for obvious reasons, I had to leave it behind. I mumbled the no-notice spell. When I was done, I said, "Ta-da." I didn't celebrate nearly as much as I should when my spells went right. It was a miracle I'd managed not to kill myself yet, and I really should take time to appreciate it.

There was the industrial estate, one of the silver metal type ones—single-storey buildings that were taller than their older brick counterparts. I grabbed my camera out of my bag, put the lens cap in my pocket, and turned the camera on. The hairs on my nape stood on end as I walked into the main driveway that serviced the complex. I knew I was unnoticeable by non-witches, but whoever was doing this was a witch, and no-notice spells didn't work on them. I didn't want to exhaust myself, but being amateurish about this now was sloppy of me. I cast a return-to-sender spell, just in case. It might drain me, drawing power for so many spells at the same time, but I wouldn't be here long.

And there it was: W & W Tea Supplies. They hadn't bothered with a proper sign. Their name was painted in black paint directly onto the metal building wall at the front. A large roller door was open, and I meandered past, pretending I was going to a different factory unit. A man drove a forklift down one of the aisles, and three other workers were packing boxes and loading them into a delivery van. It was quite the operation. Was I looking at the perpetrator right now?

Once I cleared the door, I kept walking. When I figured I was out of sight, I turned and lifted my camera. I wasn't sure exactly what I should ask for, but I may as well be direct. With the lens pointed at the front of the building but from a side view, I asked, "Show me who spelled the tea to make people violent." I held my breath.

The light changed, indicating early morning and a grey day. A man appeared in front of the warehouse, his back to me, hands on hips. He had curly reddish-blonde hair with a round thinning patch at the crown. He was not-so-stylishly dressed in a baby-poo-coloured jumper and brown slacks. I clicked off a couple of shots, but if I wanted to see him from the front, I'd have to walk past the front of the factory unit again and then turn and shoot. Best to be quick and if anyone called out, just run.

My pulse quickened, and I could feel it pounding at my throat. If the witch was here, he might very well sense what I was doing. I didn't think my talent made much of a vibration, but since I was holding other spells in place, maybe the hum was louder than normal. I wished we could hear our own spell noise. It was silly that we couldn't. I'd have to figure out how to change that. Why did I always get great ideas at the most inconvenient times? I supposed it was because that's when I needed the answers.

I walked as fast as I could without seeing where I was going in real time. The last thing I needed was to faceplant on the concrete and smash my camera. There would be nothing subtle about that. Finally next to him, I walked another few steps and made sure I stood between him and the warehouse so that when I took the shot, I faced away from the open roller door.

I turned and snapped off a few shots as I went, getting him from a kind of front side angle, and then the front. He looked to be maybe thirty or so. His fair skin was peppered with freckles, and his blonde eyebrows were wild and thick. I shivered. His gaze was focussed out of the driveway, towards the street, and straight through me.

"Hey, what are you doing?" a male voice called out from my right—from inside the warehouse, if my assumption was correct.

I turned towards the street and speed-walked while chucking my camera in my bag. Once it was safely zipped in, I slung my arms into both shoulder straps, settled my bag on my back, and ran. I didn't know if he was behind me, but in my paranoia, it felt as if a large presence was right there, looming, ready to strike.

My skin prickled, and I picked up the pace till I was sprinting back the way I'd come, my bag bouncing against my back. I held the straps at my shoulders, trying to stop everything in the knapsack being jostled too much.

Throat burning with the effort, and my legs turning to jelly, I reached the end of the street and turned left, heading for the railway station, which was still a long way away. I risked a look behind. Thank God there was no one there, except a woman getting out of her car.

I slowed, panting. Well, I hadn't looked suspicious; had

I? No, not at all. I rolled my eyes at how what I just did would have rung alarm bells with the witch responsible. Had he seen my face? Was there any way he could tell who I was? Probably not, but I didn't know all the ins and outs of witching. Anything was possible.

I recalled the vacant building with a big For Lease sign out front a little further along. As soon as I made it there, I walked down the driveway and into a sheltered doorway and dropped both the return-to-sender and no-notice spells. No way would I just hang around. The guy might be on the prowl, about to come around the corner. After glancing around to make sure no one could see me, I made my doorway and travelled home.

I couldn't wait to let James know how I'd gone. This could be the end of all the drama.

However, I forgot to say, "touch wood." I'd never been one for superstition, but maybe I needed to start.

CHAPTER 10

I let myself out of the reception room, and even though I was exhausted after holding two spells and running for my life, I ran upstairs to check on Angelica. She was where I'd left her, still asleep. Rather than waste time staring at her and worrying, I went to my room and put my bag on the bed. I took out my notepad and pen and wrote James a note. *Got photos of the guy who did it. Almost got caught, but I'm home now.* I held it up and said the words that would send it to James's pocket. The paper disappeared from between my fingers.

A few minutes later, a return note appeared in my pocket. I took it out and read. *That's great news, but I don't like that you almost got caught. Please be careful. I'll come and have a look within the next hour, as soon as I can get away.* J.

I checked my phone in case Witchface had left any

messages. Nothing from her, thank God, but Olivia had sent a message, which was fine since she knew not to say anything incriminating. *Hey, Lil. Just wanted to make sure you didn't need anything from the shops. Let me know.*

I responded. *All good, thanks. Maybe some Lavazza coffee beans. I'm all out. Just chilling here having a rest. It's been stressful lately. Thanks, Liv.* That should appeal to Agent Laaam and make her think I'd been here the whole time. Not sure if she'd buy it, but whatever.

While I waited for James, I tried not to go mad. This inevitably led to me going downstairs and turning on the TV. I sat and watched some home renovation show, my jaw clenched and my foot bobbing up and down the whole time. Witchface had my every nerve pulled tight, which irritated me because that had been part of her goal. I hated fearing her. I expected her to message a threat or carry one out at any moment. I didn't like surprises. Not. One. Bit. Unless it was Will coming over to tell me he had been faking things the whole time with Dana, and he was totally into me. Yep, I'd be waiting an eternity for that one.

On TV, they'd ripped out an old, green 1970s kitchen, except what they were replacing it with wasn't much better. I made an "ew" face at the TV. The stone benchtops were nice, but the bright red and bright purple glossy cabinet doors and disco-ball reflective-silver tiled backsplash went too far. Way too far. If that's what a designing degree made you do, I was glad I didn't have one.

I looked at my phone. Twenty minutes had passed since I'd received James's note. Argh! *Hurry up, bro.* I left my phone on the couch, jumped up and got a glass of water. My exertions this morning had made me thirsty. At least I'd burnt off that muffin. While I was downing the cool water, I realised Angelica must need something to drink. She'd been out of it since yesterday. How could I possibly get her to drink while asleep? I should really try and wake her up.

I grabbed another glass of water and went to her room whilst keeping an ear out for James, although he had a key to her reception room. I knocked, just in case, but there wasn't any answer, so I let myself in. As I approached her bed, I said, "Angelica, it's me, Lily. I've brought water. You really need to drink something."

She murmured something unintelligible but didn't open her eyes. Her bun had partly come loose of all the pins, tendrils of her hair sticking up and partly covering her face. Why hadn't I thought to take it out? It must be really uncomfortable. Before I gave her water, I did my best to untangle the mess. Her hair was soft and thankfully not knotted. Finally, it was free. "I'm sorry, Angelica. Dana did this to you. I don't know how or what she did, but she's made you very sick. I'm here to help you. Can you wake up and have a drink?"

Her lips moved slightly, and another garbled noise came out. Was she trying to speak to me, or was it just nightmare ramblings?

"I'm going to sit you up enough so that I can give you some water. Please try and swallow."

Her eyelids twitched. It probably wasn't a sign of

anything, but it was better than nothing. Maybe she could hear me and understood?

A voice filtered in from downstairs. "Lily, where are you?" James was here. Thank God.

Before I answered him, I grabbed Angelica's phone off the bedside table, made sure it was off, and shoved it in her jumper drawer, then closed it and the wardrobe door. That should muffle things if Dana had bugged it too. "I'm up here, in Angelica's room," I called back.

He was soon at the door as I struggled to get another pillow under Angelica's head to prop her up.

"What are you doing?" He stood in the doorway, eyebrows raised.

"She's been asleep since yesterday. She hasn't had anything to drink or eat since then. I'm trying to give her some water."

He strode over and stared at her. "When you said she was sick, I didn't realise you meant this sick." He ran his hand through his hair, stopping at his crown, his hand staying there. He let his hand drop, then turned to me. "And she's been like this since yesterday?"

I rolled my eyes. "Yes. I told you already. Why don't you listen the first time? Or actually take me seriously, rather. Dana has her magic in there. I have no idea what she did, but it's her fault Angelica is lying here practically dying."

"You can't prove it's Dana, though. It could be anything. Stress, overwork, lack of sleep, a virus. Anything."

I stared at my brother, the one man I loved and trusted in this world, and I had doubts about his intelligence. Why did men find it so hard to believe a beautiful woman was capable of doing something horrible? He already knew she was tampering with everyone's mind. And hell, she'd endangered Millicent and her baby. "I have proof. But it's bugged, so don't say anything while you look at it." I magicked my phone from downstairs and showed him Dana's message. When he finished looking, I sent the phone back downstairs.

"That's not definitive, Lily."

"Well, why did she message me out of the blue? I don't even have her in my contacts. She's gone to all the trouble to get my number, then taunt me about Angelica being sick."

"It's not exactly a taunt."

"Are you sure she didn't get control of your mind too?" I folded my arms and stared him down. "Have you forgotten what she did to Millicent?"

He narrowed his eyes. "No, of course not." Typical standard reaction for him to get cranky when I was right, and he didn't want to admit it.

"Can you please delve into her mind and see what's going on? Maybe don't touch anything if you think Dana will realise, but at least check it out."

He looked at me, then at Angelica. Worry lines creased his forehead. Her skin was becoming sallow, and her breathing was so faint, I could hardly tell she was alive. "She might just be sick. Why don't we call a doctor?"

"You can't be serious. What's gotten into you, James?" Argh! I wanted to scream. Couldn't he see this whole situation was too convenient?

Angelica groaned. James and I both snapped our heads

around to look at her. "Angelica? Do you need James's help?"

She groaned again. I stared at him and raised an eyebrow.

"Okay, okay."

Finally.

He placed his hands on either side of her head and concentrated. After a couple of minutes, warmth radiated from James. He pressed his lips together, and sweat shone on his forehead. I engaged my third eye and looked at him. Golden light pulsed in a halo around his body and was brightest on his hands. I could also see a faint pulse of red where he touched Angelica's head.

I reached my hands out towards James. My palms tingled and itched, then grew hot. It was as if I was getting too close to a fire. A strand of the golden energy arced across to me, the jolt stinging and shooting up my arm. I jumped back and loudly said, "No!" All my intent was on dropping my link with the power. Then the heat, the itching, all of it was gone. I was breathing hard. Had something just happened or had I imagined the whole thing?

James hadn't noticed—all his attention was rightfully on Angelica, who was moving her head from side to side slowly. Not quite thrashing, more a slow-motion version. Was he healing her or getting out the "bad" magic? And would Dana realise? Maybe she'd assume I did something. At least Millicent was out of the way and safe if that happened.

Angelica's skin was pinker than before. That had to be good, right?

James grunted, and his hands shook. Was he running out of energy? He gritted his teeth. Angelica's breathing increased, and she groaned again. What the hell was happening?

My brother's breath came in pants. He fell to his knees, dragging Angelica's head down with him, although he held his arms up as much as he could.

My scalp prickled, and I shivered. "Are you okay, James?" I put my hand on his shoulder. Could he even answer me with everything he was apparently doing? He could be in a trance for all I knew, lost in the power. Was that possible? His shoulders sagged.

I had to help, but how? Fear clawed the inside of my chest, trying to burst free. Was it possible to lend him power? He looked as if he needed it. It was as if he were straining to hold on, to give more.

I changed my focus and viewed him through my third eye. I linked myself to the river of power and concentrated on the heat pouring off him. Then I redirected the power I drew and sent it through the hand that was on his shoulder. His golden aura flared so brightly, I had to turn my head away.

The normal warmth that came with handling magic was there, only a bit hotter. And there was something new; I could actually hear the faint rushing of water. Was that the river of magic, or was I hallucinating?

James must have realised he had access to more power because he pulled at it, at me, through our link. I quickly sucked power from the river to meet his demands.

He rose from his knees until he once again stood over Angelica. Her skin was normal, a faint rose hue colouring her cheeks. She opened her eyes, awareness in them, but she quickly turned her head away from us, most likely to avoid the glare, which hadn't died down.

Did we have the normal Angelica back?

James released the power. A swarm of dizziness buzzed through my head. I swayed, then fell to the floor. I released my hold on the golden magic and shut my eyes. The steady drumbeat of a headache throbbed behind my eyeballs. Nausea played in my stomach. It was a hangover without the fun part first. Lucky me.

A moment of stillness settled over the room, and it was as if it were just me and my headache, the only sound my careful breaths tiptoeing around the pain that I sensed was ready to explode, given the right circumstances.

James's voice came from near my head. "Lily. Are you all right? What did you do?" His tone was urgent, worried, and in awe.

I whispered, "I'll be okay. Just have a headache. Want to vomit."

A small tingle radiated over my scalp. "Here's a bucket, dear, just in case." Even though I couldn't have felt crappier, I smiled. That sure sounded like the "old" Angelica.

I reached out on the opposite side of myself towards James and touched the bucket. "Thanks." I had a thousand questions to ask, but I wasn't game to move or talk much. The vomit threatening to visit the outside world needed all my effort to hold back. Gah, I hated this feeling.

I curled into a ball. All I craved was sleep. At least then I could escape this nightmare nausea.

"I think she needs to sleep, James. Can you put her in bed, please?"

"Yes, then we need to talk."

"Agreed. While you do that, I'll check the wards, and I may even add some. The recollection I have from the last week or so is hazy, but I remember how I acted, and I have my suspicions on who's to blame. You freeing me from her hold could trigger an attack. We have much to discuss. I'll see you in the sitting room."

As James carried me to my room, he said, "I'm not exactly sure what you did back there, Lily, but don't tell anyone. If you had a price on your head before, triple that, then quadruple that, and then you might come close to what you're worth to those people now."

Great. More reason to worry. As if I wasn't stressed enough.

James lowered me onto my bed, and I lifted my legs and got under the covers. "Thanks," I mumbled. "Will Angelica be okay?"

"I'm pretty sure she's back to normal, thanks to you."

"And you."

"Just get some sleep. I'm sure you have lots of questions, and I'll answer them when you wake up. Millicent is safe at her parents', and after what just happened, I think I'll stay tonight so I'll be here when you wake up." He stroked my head, then left, shutting my door after himself.

I managed to hold off vomiting long enough to drift off to sleep.

The last thought I had before going under was that Angelica had mentioned an attack. There was only one person she could be talking about.

Dana.

When the nightmares came, I had no strength to wake.

CHAPTER 11

When I woke, it was still dark. A quick look at my phone, which someone had kindly put on my bedside table, showed it was 4:50 a.m. I rubbed the discomfort at my side, under my arm. Argh. I'd gone to bed fully clothed, and that meant bra. Sleeping while cocooned in underwire was not a pleasant experience.

I considered trying to go back to sleep—it was way too early to get up—but I was wide awake. That's what happened when you went to bed in the afternoon. Thankfully, the nausea and headache had disappeared, but the gloomy shadows of my nightmares remained.

Eager to shake off the feeling of dread, I got up and tiptoed downstairs. It was too early for a shower—I'd wake everyone. In the kitchen, I grabbed a glass of water. Ooh, there was a gold-coloured packet on the counter. I smiled. Olivia had returned safely and baring coffee grounds.

I turned the coffee machine on, filled the thingy with coffee, and inserted it into its home on the machine. I wasn't magicking anything this morning—my body needed a break. My limbs were heavy and sore, as if I'd run a marathon yesterday. I'd spend time later stretching because at least some of the ache had come from the sprint I'd done. Even though running was part of my regular routine, I'd pushed myself hard yesterday, not to mention all the magic use. The combination was ridiculously painful.

Coffee made, I opened the back door and sat on the park bench—the same one I'd sat on at James's welcome-home party after being kidnapped. The same one where James had given me our mother's diaries. What would she think of our current situation? I had no doubt she would have protected us and given us some great advice.

I sipped my coffee and watched through thick jasmine-scented air as the sky lightened, painting the smattering of clouds coral. I hugged my arms to my sides and cradled my cup to my chest. Such calm and serenity, almost like being in the eye of the storm, except birds chirped and squirrels darted along branches in the large tree whose thick branches reached over our back fence.

Soft footsteps shuffled behind me. "Hey."

I turned and smiled. "Hey, big bro."

He sat next to me, dark hair scruffy, his jaw sporting five o'clock shadow, although I didn't think five in the morning was the time they meant. He put his forearms on his legs and turned his head towards me. "How are you feeling?"

"I'm much better, thanks. Remember the last time we were sitting out here?"

"Seems like a lifetime ago."

"Tell me about it. I'm sure not the same person who came here at the end of April."

He grinned. "You can say that again." He gestured, and the familiar tingle of magic warmed my scalp. "Bubble of silence."

I nodded. "How's Angelica?"

"Free of Dana's influence. That witch did a real number on her. The more Angelica fought it, the more it tried to infiltrate her brain. It would have killed her or made her pretty much brain dead. I've never seen anything like it. She'd trapped it, so it fought my attempts to destroy it." He shook his head. "I've never seen anything like that either. It's crazy. If it wasn't for you giving me your power, I would have died or given up." He stared at me, worry and confusion playing over his face. "How did you do it, Lily? It's supposed to be impossible."

I returned his stare with one of blankness. "I have no idea. When I look at witches with my third eye, I don't just see their aura. I can also feel the heat from their magic—at least, that's where I figure it's from. It's not just body heat, but something that's generated with a kind of vibration as well. It's hard to describe. I once felt it with Will, and he shut down the conversation and basically left."

James stared into the distance at the sky, which had brightened, the darkness giving way to faded blue. We sat in silence for a couple of minutes, and when he spoke, he didn't move, just kept staring at the vast cloud-smattered blue. "If you can give power, you can draw it too. In our history books, there has only ever been one witch like you. She lived over a thousand years ago. When the witch ruling council at the time found out what she could do, they killed her."

The birds chirped. The squirrels squirrelled. My stomach dropped, and my mouth went dry. Why couldn't I be a bird or squirrel? Life would go on as per normal. Maybe I could change myself into one? Hmm, I'd have to look into it. As a squirrel, I could do cute things and become an Internet sensation, plus I liked nuts. Nuts were good food, and if I begged, I was sure humans would feed me chocolate muffins and coffee.

"Well, Lily? Say something." He finally turned to look at my face.

"I don't know what to say. Should I just kill myself and avoid weeks or months of thinking someone will murder me any moment?"

"No! Of course not."

"I don't even know if I can draw power from someone else, and if I can, we just won't tell anyone. Does Angelica know?"

"Yes, she does. We've been discussing the best way to utilise your talents against Dana without anyone knowing. I'm not sure it can be done, though."

Ooh, we were planning to overthrow queen of the piranhas. I liked the sound of that. "Surely any witch could see me transferring power to you if they looked with their other sight."

"Yep, and we can't risk it. Anyway, we can beat Dana without it, but we have to tread carefully. She has everyone at the PIB enthralled, which is no small thing. The energy she'd need to keep it going is almost unthinkable."

"Remember that day at the art gallery—you mentioned some kind of cloaking device? Would that help her draw and hold a lot of power without killing herself from the effort? Because, let me tell you, if I'd gone on much longer yesterday, I might have died. I was totally drained afterwards. It really showed me how weak I really am. I have no witch stamina." They needed a witch gym, where you could go to build up your magic muscles. Hmm, better not advertise it like that. "Magic muscles" was a bit ambiguous. I snickered.

He looked at me as if I'd gone mad. "And that's totally hilarious."

"I wasn't laughing about that. Never mind. So, what if it is some kind of illegal witchy device. How do we find it and destroy it?"

"I have no idea. Why don't we wait for Angelica to get up, and we can have a proper meeting—the three of us. There's also the not-so-small matter of the witch who spelled violence on Westerham and Kent. I had a look through your camera, and I've done some research. The guy's name is Gabriel Whitehorse. He grew up in Westerham, went to a local school. His father's dead and his mother's in a special nursing home for witches."

Oh, wow. I had no idea there were special ones for witches. I wondered if they came with extra security— demented witches could probably cause a lot of trouble. You'd need more than a passcode to keep them in. Maybe the whole place was warded? On a good note, if you worked there, you could just magic the cleaning, nappy changes, and sponge baths.

"Do you have any ideas on why he did it?" Why would someone want to do something so heinous—pit neighbour against neighbour, sibling against sibling, and partners against each other?

"I haven't gotten that far. I'll have to interview people who knew him. I'm still digging, trying to find his old school friends, find out where he worked before running the tea business. Come on. Let's go inside. I'm going to cook some breakfast. How do pancakes sound?"

"With whipped cream and strawberries?" I wasn't an early-morning eater, but for that, I'd make an exception.

"Sure. Why not?"

There was one sip of coffee left in my cup, and I swallowed it. Argh! It was cold. I stood and waved at the squirrels. "See you later, little cuties. Maybe I'll join you later in squirrel form." I grinned. Life goals: becoming a squirrel. It was the best idea I'd had in a while.

By the time I stepped into the kitchen, James had the table set and was magicking up the pancakes. Three plates, a bowl of strawberries, and a bowl of cream all waited. I sat at the table just as Angelica walked through the door, dressed and impeccable, her hair back in its bun. I smiled. "Welcome back."

She smiled. "I could say the same to you. How are you feeling?" She sat opposite me, and a steaming cup of tea appeared on the table in front of her.

"I'm good. A bit sore and tired, but nothing permanent. What about you? Are you… Um. Do you hate me?"

She shook her head slowly, her face sad. "I'm so sorry, Lily. Dana's powers of persuasion are stronger than any of us realised. Before I knew what had happened, she had control of my mind. There was part of me, buried deep, that was aghast at what I was saying and allowing to happen to you. Can you forgive me?"

"There's nothing to forgive. It wasn't your fault."

"I should have realised she was unhinged when she returned. In fact, when she left for New York, after she broke Will's heart, I held some ill will towards her. She hadn't conducted herself with as much empathy as I would have liked. It told me a lot about who she was, but I shrugged it off, told myself she was one of our best agents, and that the PIB needed all kinds to function."

"By all kinds, do you mean someone needs to work the torture chamber?" I laughed because I was joking. The look Angelica gave me, lips pressed together, eyes serious told me I was close to the truth. "Oh, crap."

"Sometimes it takes what it takes."

"But that's barbaric!"

"Lily, if you'd seen some of the witches we've seen, you would know not everyone readily admits to the horrors they've perpetrated, and sometimes we need that extra incentive. What we do is for the good of the world, for mankind, and witches. That kind of thing is not common, and it's not something I'm proud of. More an evil necessity."

I trusted her, and I knew what she was saying made sense—when you were dealing with evil, a decent person was automatically not on a level playing field. The question was: What were we willing to sacrifice to keep everyone safe?

I looked from Angelica to my brother. "Is there a bubble of silence around us?" We'd been talking about Dana, and from the conversation, it was clear Angelica was better and ready to fight. I hoped someone had thought to keep it private.

Angelica answered, "Yes, of course. I set one as soon as I sat down. Dana may have had control of me for a while, but I'm back, and I'm ready to take her down, all the way to the PIB cells." She smiled.

I grinned. She would so enjoy living there. I could vouch for the disgustingness of their toilets and how boring it was. Knowing she was in there was going to bring me so much joy, and if that made me a horrible person, I would be glad to wear that tag. "I'm happy to hear it. So, how do we go about that?"

James put the pancakes on the table and sat next to me. Mmm, they smelled delicious. I stabbed one with my fork and put it on my plate. "Thanks. These look awesome."

"My pleasure. Angelica and I had a chat while you were asleep. The first thing we need to do is prove that Gabriel had a motive, which means we need to dig into his past. Angelica and I are going to do that without alerting Dana and Drake. Drake is obviously in Dana's control, but Angelica is still a higher rank than Dana, so the only thing stopping us from investigating is Drake ordering us to stay away, and if he doesn't know what we're doing, he can't make that order. So, we have to tread carefully. After we establish his motive, we'll need to prove he did it, of course. We can't use your photos, so we're going to have to figure out how he did it and come up with some proof. We also may need you to take more photos to help us find the direction we need to go. Are you up for that, Lily?"

"Yes. Definitely." I didn't have to think twice. This was going to be dangerous, but that wasn't anything different from what my life was anyway. Plus, Dana being free to run the PIB would create more danger than what I was currently experiencing, truth be told. I was all in.

I covered my pancake with strawberries and smothered it all in cream and took a bite. Sooooo delicious.

"What about the gadget she might have that helps her do magic quietly?" If I knew what it was, maybe I could get it off her at some point.

Angelica placed her teacup on the saucer. "I've been thinking about that. If you use a magic cloaking device, you have to be touching it the entire time you draw magic for the spell. She wears a gold band on the middle finger of her right hand. It would either be that, her diamond stud earrings, or maybe she has something strapped to her body. She doesn't wear a necklace—which I know because she rarely wears a tie and has her three top shirt buttons undone." Angelica sighed and shook her head. I was glad I wasn't the only one who thought she was an attention-seeking witch.

"So it's not going to be easy getting it off her."

James shook his head. "Unless you want to try chopping her hand off when she least expects it."

Angelica laughed. "I can see it now. First we chop off her hand, but that's not it, so we have to chop off her ears, but that's not it. I wonder what else we might have to do?"

James snickered. Oh my God. Typical Angelica. She loved gruesome. Every. Single. Time. I shook my head, although my mouth twitched up. It was kind of funny, but only because I knew she was joking. Hmm… "You are joking, aren't you?"

Angelica and James looked at each other, then looked at me. They both burst out laughing. Okaaaay. That was not an answer. I gave up.

Angelica settled down and took a sip of tea, then said, "Don't worry, dear. We'll worry about the amulet, or whatever it is, later. First we need to make our case against Gabriel. Don't forget: there are still violent crimes going on out there, and thousands of people's lives have been upended. We need to stop that before we do anything else, or who knows how far it will spread."

"Of course. I know. I'm so glad we have you back. I missed you." I forked some cream-laden pancake into my mouth.

Angelica smiled. "It's good to be back. Now, enjoy your

breakfast, dears, because, after this, we'll have to get to work. And our job won't be easy."

Argh, as if I needed *that* reminder.

I savoured every bite of pancake. Who knew—maybe it would be the last time we all ate together? I wasn't prone to morbid thoughts, but Dana was out for blood, and I had a feeling I was first on her list.

CHAPTER 12

I looked at my phone for the tenth time in fifteen minutes. It was 8:12 p.m., and James and Angelica were overdue. They'd been out interviewing and chasing leads all day, and we were potentially going to visit the warehouse tonight, get inside, and see what we could find. To distract myself, I'd grabbed Olivia, and we were watching TV in the downstairs living room.

"Oh, my God! Lily, it's William!"

My heart spasmed, then raced as my head shot up from my phone. "What? Where?"

"There!" She'd jumped to her feet and was animatedly pointing at the television. "Look!"

I leaned forward. "Oh, God." He was standing with another agent, two police officers, and four men in army gear, attempting to hold back a mob in Canterbury. The violence had finally spread. Crap. The crowd was blocking the tourist entry to Canterbury Cathedral grounds. The whole road was filled with people yelling abuse and throwing bottles, shoving and punching each other, but they were also advancing on William's group. A bottle flew towards his head. He hit it out of the way at the last second.

Crap.

"Bloody hell, Liv! Is that Dana standing next to him?" The camera had been filming from the side, and whilst I saw the matching suit to Will's, I hadn't seen the agent's face. Now that the camera panned around more from the front, their identity was revealed. "Turn it up."

She turned it up, and the jeering got louder. A chant started. "Kill the pigs. Kill the pigs." A chair flew past the camera and hit one of the soldiers in the shoulder. He stumbled backwards but kept his feet. Where the hell did someone get a chair?

The male reporter off-camera said in a harried voice, "The situation is deteriorating. Army backup has been called, but they haven't arrived."

A call of, "Charge!" came from the masses, and I swear to God, Dana smiled. Did she know the camera was filming her? Oh, apparently she did because she looked straight at it. Then all hell broke loose. The crowd surged. Dana shoved Will to the ground. She pointed at the camera, and the picture went black, but in the split second before it did, Dana disappeared.

My breath was coming fast. "Did you see that, Liv? Did you see she disappeared?"

Her mouth had fallen open, and she nodded.

"I have to get to Will. He'll be trampled to death." My thoughts raced, as unruly as the mob had been.

The newsroom came on, and the attractive blonde behind the desk apologised for the loss of picture.

"I'm going, Liv. If Angelica and James get back, tell them where I am. I'll do my best to get Will back here as soon as I can." I pulled the mind map up in my head and focussed on Canterbury—I'd been there only three weeks ago on a day trip. The cathedral was magnificent, and I had the photos of stained glass and soaring ceilings to prove it. There was a witch's landing place nearby, in Burgate public toilets.

My map dissolved as Liv spoke. "You can't go. What if something happens to you? What if it's a trap?" Lines were set into her brow—when those lines appeared, it meant there was little chance she'd be swayed.

"How can it be a trap? She couldn't know I was watching this channel, or that they'd even televise it. Just because there was a news crew there doesn't mean it would make the news. There must be hundreds of them out there filming different things."

"I just have a funny feeling."

My mouth went dry. "The more we argue, the more danger Will is in. I can't let him die." I tuned out her voice and brought the map up again. I pinpointed where I wanted to go, stamped the coordinates on my door, and stepped through.

Ew, the toilets stank. I burst out of the door and turned right. Soon, I hit a T-intersection with Burgate Street. I turned right and kept running. Déjà vu anyone? I turned left at the next street, which was wider and busier. Screams and shouts, cries of anger rippled towards me. I mumbled a return-to-sender spell, just in case Dana was hanging around.

Smoke smudged the air. It burnt my throat as I did my best to gulp in oxygen to feed my sprinting legs. I was almost at the cathedral. Hundreds of crazed humans filled the road. Some had broken from where the bodies were thickest, and they were smashing shop windows, grabbing what they could, and running, or waiting for someone else to do it, and then punching them, taking the stuff and running.

Holy hell. This was bad. And where was Will?

I slowed to a walk and coughed. My eyes watered from the smoke. I dragged my black T-shirt over my mouth and nose—I'd changed into black jeans and T-shirt in readiness for our foray to the warehouses later.

A group of people had formed a circle and were taking turns kicking whoever was on the ground in the middle of it. There was no way that person would survive if this went on much longer. Was it Will? Nausea demanded I vomit in the gutter, but I ignored it. There wasn't time to freak out now. If I needed to vomit, I'd do it later.

Someone howled; then another took up the call. I was pretty sure no one was about to turn into a werewolf, but you never knew.

I reached the group. "Stop. What are you doing? Stop!"

They ignored me. I bent over, trying to see in between

the people. One man growled, another swore, a woman's voice screamed, "Kill the bastard!"

I tried to pry a shorter man from the circle, but he didn't budge, didn't even turn and look at me. There was no way I was going to achieve anything without magic.

Someone slammed into me from behind, and I crashed into the guy I'd just tried to pull out of the circle. He flew forward and tripped over whoever was on the ground, then hit the person opposite him in the circle as he went down. I'd managed to stop myself from falling, or he'd stopped me, probably. I turned to see who had tried to push me over, but no one was there. Was it Dana, or had whoever pushed me just moved on to hurt someone else?

The rest of the people in the circle, distracted by the kerfuffle, broke into three separate groups and started beating the crap out of each other. I knelt carefully next to what I could now see was a man. He wore camouflage—he must be one of the army personnel. Where were his comrades? Surely they wouldn't leave one of their own to die. Either they were busy fighting for their own lives, or they didn't realise he'd fallen. I checked for a pulse. His face was bloody, his nose bent to the side. I winced. That must have hurt.

I felt a faint beat in his neck. Okay, so far so good. He was alive, but where was Will, and who could I get to help me? Oh crap. I felt in my back pocket. My phone was in there. If Dana wasn't already here, she would surely be here any moment. I turned and looked around. Despite my luck being normally bad, about twenty army personnel were jogging in unison towards us. I stood and called out, waving my arm. "Over here! A fallen soldier. Over here!"

Two of the men broke away and ran faster, reaching me quickly. They thanked me and took over. Soon the other soldiers arrived and started hitting people to the ground and handcuffing them. I didn't know if that was their usual protocol, but scary times called for new measures. Whatever it took to survive.

I stood. Where was Will?

"I thought I told you to stay home."

If it wasn't for making sure Will was okay, I'd have made my door and been home in an instant. I took a deep breath and turned to face Dana. "You can stick your orders up your a—"

She pressed her finger against my lips. "Tsk, tsk. Is that any way to speak to the acting chief of the PIB?" Oh crap —the acting chief.

I wanted to bite her finger off, but I was afraid her blood would poison me. I grabbed her wrist instead and pulled her hand down while I digested this new information. We were in so much trouble.

I didn't want to buy into her chatter, but I had to ask. "What happened to Drake?"

"He must have caught the same thing poor Ma'am caught. I think he even has a worse case of it. Quite ill, I'm afraid."

I still had her wrist. Was it the same side as the ring? I risked looking down. It was! Without taking any time to think about it, I pressed my fingers around it and tugged.

The metal was so cold it burned, searing my thumb and pointer finger. She snatched her hand away. If she hadn't, I might have let go anyway. That had bloody hurt. It still stung.

"I didn't peg you for a thief, petal. I could have you jailed for that." For the briefest moment, surprise lit her eyes, but then she was as poker-faced as the best PIB agent, namely Angelica.

"You have no authority over me. Where's Will?" I was beyond caring about her threats. She would do what she wanted, whether I disobeyed her or not, and Millicent was safe.

She smirked. "Wouldn't you love to know?"

I narrowed my eyes, anger percolating in my blood, energising me more than even coffee could. "Where is he?"

"Somewhere you'll never find him, at least for now." She put her hand around my throat and squeezed hard enough to make it uncomfortable. I grabbed her wrist, but she was too strong, surprising since she was so slim, but she was probably trained in hand-to-hand combat. Why didn't I think of these things before I antagonised evil people? "You think you're so clever, getting Millicent out of my way, but now I have William. Anymore interfering, and I'll kill him."

My eyes widened. "But you love him… or at least what passes for love in your psychotic mind. You wouldn't."

She smiled, and the pleasure in her eyes chilled my blood, making me shiver. "Nothing and nobody gets in my way when I want something. I would have killed you by now, but it's not allowed… yet." Her smile mutated into a snarl.

What did she mean by that? And if she wasn't allowed to kill me, how was she allowed to kill William?

Her gaze zoned out as if she were listening to someone else. Then she refocused her cruel stare on me. "William is merely a tool, and I will kill him and deliver his body to you as punishment."

I tried to put on a poker face, willed my feelings to stay in the back of my mind, but it was a skill at which I sorely lacked. She laughed.

"You've been warned. Now go home. If I see you out of the house again, you'll be responsible for William's death. Do you understand?"

I squeezed her wrist harder, trying to remove it. She probably hadn't zapped me again because I had the return-to-sender spell up. I drew on my power and looked at her with my third eye. She had that spell up as well, so she shouldn't have been afraid of my spell—I was weaker than her. And strangely, her aura was the colour of tarnished copper—still glowing, even pretty, but darker. And she didn't radiate heat. A fog of frigid air flowed off her, as if she were a block of dry ice. It made me think of the typical roiling vapour that movies always had coming out of black caul-drons. If she didn't have her hand around my throat, I might have laughed.

"Do. You. Understand?" she asked through gritted teeth, her fingers squeezing harder.

I struggled to take a breath, then released her wrist and tried to force the fingers of both my hands under her hand, to pry it off. But she was too strong. I wanted to punch her in the face, but instead, I nodded. Man, it galled me to do that, but to get rid of her for good, we had to play the long game. I was pretty sure that punching her would just lead to more pain, and it would likely be mine.

"Say it!"

My voice was uneven as I fought the lack of air and the pressure around my neck. "I understand."

"Good, petal. Now go home. Oh, and when you get there, you can tell Angelica that next time she comes in, she's fired for attempting to undermine her superiors. I run the PIB now. Everyone answers to me. Time to go, petal. I'll count it down for you." She snatched her hand from around my neck, and I stumbled forward. "Five... four..."

I ground my back teeth together and made my doorway.

"Three... two..."

I stepped through, fists clenched.

But we weren't done.

No. Freaking. Way.

CHAPTER 13

I stepped out of Angelica's reception room and locked the door. I turned to walk back to the TV room and find Olivia, but she was running towards me. Then she was in front of me, gripping my arms. "Lily! Are you okay? Oh my God, what were you thinking? We've been so worried about you." I looked over her shoulder. Shaking his head, James stood in the doorway to the sitting room.

"I'm fine. Hang on a sec." I turned my phone off and made a bubble of silence. "I had my phone with me, idiot that I am, and Dana found me. I couldn't see Will anywhere. Dana says she has him somewhere we'll never find him, and that if I leave the house again, she'll kill him."

Olivia dropped her hands from my arms. "She would never kill him. She loves him... doesn't she?"

"No. She was just using him. It seems to be how she operates."

"And he knows all that." James folded his arms. "Come in here, ladies. There are a few things we need to discuss." He turned and led the way.

Huh? Was this about to get interesting? We filed in. Olivia sat next to Angelica, who was already seated on the Chesterfield facing me, and James sat on the other one. I sat next to him.

"So." I turned to face James. "You said he already knows. Does he love her, or have the past few weeks been an act?" As much as I didn't want to want Will, I couldn't help it. Was I about to get the answer I'd been desperate for since Witchface had arrived?

"Of course they've been an act. But as much as he tried to protect himself from her persuasion, he's under her control now. I didn't realise what was happening until you told me."

I let out the breath I'd been holding. It didn't mean he wanted to date me, but at least there was a chance. He didn't love that scheming, evil witch.

Angelica removed invisible fluff from her black PIB trousers. "She does it so gradually; you don't hear or see it coming. Like that frog in the boiling water analogy, although it's not true. Unfortunately, we're not frogs, and Dana is more subtle than hot water."

"I'm also supposed to pass on a message to you, Ma'am." I used her PIB title because she was the boss there as far as I was concerned. "She said you're fired—"

Olivia's abrupt intake of breath matched Angelica's face. Although Angelica's expression was there and gone so quickly that if I'd blinked, I would have missed it. Her face relaxed, but her eyes told a different story. Fury pulsed in her eyes, coiled and ready to strike. I couldn't wait until she unleashed it all over Dana's smug self.

"She also said that everyone at the PIB answers to her now. She's sidelined Drake with whatever you had, although I think he's in worse condition, and I imagine no one is helping him." How would Angelica play this? Would she let him perish as his brain lost all semblance of self under Dana's relentless stripping away of his beliefs, thoughts, and desires? The war that waged in his mind would burn him out if it went on long enough, if Angelica's ordeal was anything to go by.

Or would she try and save him?

I wasn't against saving him, but I'd rather save Will first, and Beren, although I didn't know how entrenched she was in his brain. Maybe she'd only done enough to sway him to her side. Although, I doubted it. Beren was kind, but he wasn't stupid or naïve.

"She's out of control," said James. "Unfortunately, we can't deal with her until we've got enough evidence on Gabriel. If Angelica can beat her to the punch, it will infuriate her, maybe get her to make a mistake. Taking her down will take some planning. I have no doubt she has the full support of everyone at the PIB. We're going to have to figure out a way to render her mind control useless."

"I tried to take the ring off her tonight, and she didn't like it. I'm pretty sure that's the device she's using. It was freezing to the point of burning my fingers." I held my hand up. The top pads of my thumb and pointer finger were crimson, and a blister had formed on my finger.

James grabbed my hand and inspected my digits closely. "That looks painful. I think it's safe to assume that's what she's using to channel and silence her magic. Hold on for a sec, Lil." He gently touched his fingers to the burnt spots. Warmth spread from his fingers to mine, and the painful throb faded away to nothing. He released my fingers. They were back to normal—no redness and no blisters.

"Thank you." I smiled.

"It's what big brothers do." He winked.

"I want a big brother," said Olivia.

I laughed. "You can borrow mine if you want. That's okay; isn't it, James?"

"Ha, totally."

Olivia's expression turned serious, her brows drawing down. "How's Beren doing with all of this?"

In the chaos, I'd forgotten she *liked* him. Not that she'd ever been upfront about it, but I could tell—the same way she could tell I was into Will before I'd admitted it.

Angelica answered. "The last time I saw him, he was well enough. I think this whole thing has confused him. Things are hazy from the last week or so, but some moments have stuck with me. Drake had ordered everyone out to help manage the chaos, and then Dana spoke up and said, no, it's not necessary. Beren's confusion was on his face. He was going to say something, but then he shut his mouth and nodded slowly, as if he were just realising, yes, that was the best way. And instead of arguing, I was thinking it made sense for us to not get involved, leave the non-witches to themselves. The fact that we're supposed to protect them from witch crime didn't even cross my mind. She has control over him, but not to the same degree as she had over me, or Drake."

James twisted his wedding ring around his finger. "Even with that device she has, she's spreading herself thin. She wouldn't be able to have the same strength of influence with everyone. She may even just focus it when she needs someone to make a decision in her favour."

I slid to the edge of the seat and sat up straighter. "So, first thing is to go to the warehouse tonight and gather more evidence. Then we come back here and figure out our next move." I looked at Angelica. "Did you find anything helpful today in terms of Gabriel's motivation?"

She smiled. "Oh, yes. All four people we interviewed from his school days were non-witches. They admitted he was teased mercilessly. Everyone thought he was crazy because he kept bragging that he was a witch, which, of course, is a big no-no."

"First rule of witch club...." I giggled, and James grinned.

Angelica raised her brow, then continued, "He stopped short of doing magic, except for one unexplained case of two of the bullies coming down with a full-body rash of unknown origin for two days. Apparently the children scratched until they bled. We interviewed his sole friend from high school who admitted even he found him weird. He also used to threaten to destroy Westerham and the people who were so cruel to him when he left school. I'd say that's his motivation."

Inside me, a flutter of sympathy took off, but it was quickly smacked down by the cat's paw of consequences—he knew bragging about his origins was forbidden, yet he did it anyway, and it was probably to show off. Not that I condoned any kind of bullying, but surely he knew he was courting trouble by declaring he was a witch? I mean, that was the whole reason we kept it a secret—because of perse-cution. It would be awesome if the world wasn't that way, if differences were accepted and celebrated. Imagine what the good witches could do if non-witches appreciated us? We could make their lives so much easier.

My mouth dropped open. Could Beren cure cancer? Imagine all the people he could save, all the children. Mind. Blown. Maybe we should work towards coming out to the world.

"Lily. Earth to Lily. Come in, Lily." James was waving his hand in front of my face.

"Oh, sorry." I gave him a sheepish grin. "You know how I am…."

James shook his head and sighed. "Yes, unfortunately, we do."

"Hey!" I play-punched him in the arm.

"Okay, children, back to work." One corner of Angeli-ca's mouth was turned up just enough to take the firmness out of her words.

James reached into a black bag at his feet. How had I not noticed it before? I wasn't very observant. He pulled out two bulky, black phone-looking things with thick aerials. I laughed. "Are those walkie-talkies?" Mum and Dad had given us cheap ones when we were kids, and we used to play spies. Those were the days, when it was only make-believe.

"Yes, dear sister, they are. We'll have one, but try not to use it when we're sneaking around. It's more for an emergency situation to contact Olivia, who is going to be our base manager." He handed her one and smiled, then handed me the other.

"I get to help? Wow, thanks!" Olivia grinned and inspected her gadget.

"If things go pear-shaped and we can't get out for whatever reason, call Olivia. She's going to call my mate who's a sergeant in the army, and he'll get some guys down there. He's a non-witch who knows about us. Two of his team also know about us, and the rest—well, we'll just wipe their memories if it comes to that. I've warned him that I may need assistance later, but I haven't given him any details, for obvious reasons." He showed me what buttons to press to call Olivia. Then he got up and sat next to Olivia to show her. He then pulled out a piece of paper. "If we call and ask you to get help, use your mobile phone to call my friend on this number. Tell him your name is Susan Smith, and he'll know it's about me. Give him these coordinates." James pointed to a spot on the paper. "Got it?"

She nodded. "Yep. All good." Olivia looked at me and gave me an oh-my-God-this-is-awesome look. I grinned. When she passed her exams and joined the police and PIB, she'd be working with James more often. That was, *if* we won. If we lost, there was no way Olivia would want to work with the PIB, and what about Angelica and James? Surely they'd lose their jobs, not to mention, there's no way they'd compromise their principals and work for a lying, law-breaking psychopath. Gee, there was more on the line than I'd figured. I didn't care if I didn't work for them since I was only a contractor, but for everyone else in my life, it was their livelihoods, their passion.

I stood, handed Olivia my phone, and magicked my camera into my hand. "Are we ready?"

Everyone stood. "Good luck, guys. You got this." Olivia looked at each of us in turn.

Angelica turned to me. "I'm sending you the coordinates. I snuck by earlier and set a temporary doorway position that will last for forty-eight hours. It comes out in the complex next door, at the side of the building where there is no light and no surveillance camera. When you come out, just follow me. James will go first, and we'll wait sixty seconds for him to make sure there is no one inside our target building and disarm the security cameras and alarm. If there is someone there, he'll contact us on the walkie-talkie. We have plans for either scenario, so just follow my lead with as little talk as possible. Got it?"

I nodded. "Yes. Follow you. No talking."

Golden coordinates appeared in my mind. I made my doorway, stuck them on, then stepped through.

It was dark. Not pitch, but close. I'd been last to arrive, and James was already out of sight. He hadn't wasted any time. Angelica stood at the end of the little alleyway created by the side of the brick warehouse and the brick fence. I quietly joined her and slid the walkie-talkie into my back pocket. Distant traffic noise droned, and an owl hooted. The cool night air had me wishing I'd worn my cardie. Goose-bumps peppered my arms, and I rubbed one arm.

I placed a return-to-sender spell on myself, removed my lens cap, and shoved it in my other back pocket. My camera cord was around my neck, and my thumb was ready to flick the On switch.

The wait felt like forever. It was like having a boring job and watching the clock—time definitely went slower when you didn't want it to. Another way the universe was actively screwing with us. Stupid universe.

Where was Will? Was he okay? I bit my lip. What if Witchface knew I was out and was killing him right now? I swallowed and fought the need to throw up. *Don't think about it. Focus on what you're doing, Lily.*

I shut my eyes momentarily and pictured his face as he stared at me through the rear-view mirror. God, I missed him. I opened my eyes and started counting. One penguin, two penguins, three penguins… I got to twenty-three when Angelica finally took off. She turned right. It wasn't far from the driveway to the footpath, where we turned left, and then it was only fifteen metres to the driveway I'd so recently run out of in panic.

We reached the door to Gabriel's factory unit. James held the door open and motioned us inside. Angelica slipped past him and turned left into the main warehouse area. I flicked my camera on and followed. As I entered, Angelica turned on the light and gave me a thumbs-up gesture. I nodded and positioned myself with my back against the main warehouse roller door. Shelving started about a quarter of the way down the high-clearance room, creating three aisles. Boxes took up every available space on the shelves.

Angelica had donned rubber gloves. She slid one box from a bottom-level shelf and opened it. She scooped out a handful of what I assumed were tea leaves. Warmth rolled down the back of my neck as she stared at the contents of her hand. Likely satisfied she had evidence, she pulled a plastic bag out of her pocket and filled it. Then she picked another box from further down the row and started again.

I walked to the beginning of the aisle to my left, my sneakers squeaking on the polished concrete. Lifting my camera to my face, I looked through the viewfinder. "Show me if Gabriel has any accomplices in his scheme to spell the tea to turn the Westerham inhabitants violent."

Nothing in the first aisle. I moved across to the second, then the third. Nothing. Without lowering my camera, I turned to the door we'd used that led from off the little entryway.

Well, this was interesting.

Gabriel, facing me, had his hand in the air, gesticulating. His open mouth was obviously in the middle of saying something. Two people stood with their backs to me—a tall, dark-haired man wearing a short-sleeved purple collared shirt, and a petite black-haired woman who was short compared to him, but she was at least my height. He had a muscly, tattooed arm around her slim waist. She leaned into him, but her arms were folded.

I approached them, snapping shots as I walked around and behind Gabriel. When I saw the faces of the two people Gabriel was talking to, I gasped. I shouldn't have been surprised, though. The woman was none other than Dana Piranha, aka, Witchface, or my favourite, Agent Laaam. She had her PIB uniform on, and that ring was in place. Was the guy her boyfriend?

The guy with the questionable taste in girlfriends looked to be in his forties and had an olive complexion and brown eyes. If I had to guess, I'd say Greek. He had a thick gold chain around his neck. Ew. I wasn't a fan of men in jewellery. He had three- or four-day growth happening, and his left earlobe was missing. Okaaaay. Had it been bitten off, or was he born like that? A snake tattoo wrapped around his neck, the letters *ISSAM* in golden scrollwork forming the end of its tail. I looked closer, under his jaw. There was another word in golden scrollwork that said, *REGULA*. Was that some weird rap name, or did he have shares in a laxative company and couldn't spell? Maybe I could put this picture on Facebook later with a tattoo-fail hashtag. I snorted.

I took close-ups of the tattoos. Shame I couldn't take his shirt off and see what other tats he had. Not because I wanted to see him semi-naked, but maybe they'd give us a clue as to who he was. Maybe his face would show up in PIB records?

And then there was Dana. Had she orchestrated this

scheme, or had Gabriel just paid her to keep the PIB out of it? Was this about money and power? *Ha ha, Lily. Stupid question.* Wasn't most dodgy stuff about that? Silly me. Again.

Without telling anyone what I'd found, I went upstairs. Maybe I could find additional information that would let us know her motive, as well as the identity of that guy. According to my magic, he was involved too. He wasn't just arm candy. My camera would have likely shown me a different scenario with just Gabriel and Dana, or just Dana herself, if that guy wasn't involved. As much as things had been hit-and-miss when I first started, whenever I asked to see something, it was usually accurate, even if I couldn't figure out how at the time.

I had no doubt these three were in it together. I just didn't know who was running things.

I reached the landing. There were two doors to choose from off the short hallway. One to the left, and one straight ahead. The door to the left was open. Footsteps came from inside. I tensed. Then James appeared at the door. "Lily? What's wrong?"

I huffed out a huge breath. Thank God. "I heard a noise and thought we might be busted, but it's only you."

"*Only* me? Gee, thanks." His lopsided grin told me he was kidding.

"That *only* was said with much relief, I'll have you know. Have you found anything?"

"Yep. Supply receipts, all on paper. Maybe they didn't want the proof to be a forever kind of thing. It would be easy to burn all this when they were done."

"Are you going to copy it or take it? I imagine we don't want them to know we've been here until they've been arrested."

"I'm copying each sheet as I find it with just a wave of my hand. The copied receipts are sitting in boxes at Angelica's."

"Nice work."

"What about you?" He pointed to my camera.

"Getting there. I just want to finish up here before I tell you what I found."

He raised a brow. "If you're keeping me in suspense, it better be good news."

I smiled. "You'll see." He he. I enjoyed teasing him. "Okay, bro. Out of my way so I can get this done. Then I'll spill."

He stepped out of my way and back to one of two filing cabinets against the wall to my left. I stood just inside the doorway. "Show me who came up with the idea for the tea-spelling operation in Westerham." Gabriel appeared, sitting at a desk. He was alone. I clicked a couple of frames, then photographed the papers on his desk.

"Now show me who's in charge of the tea-spelling operation." I expected Dana to appear after what I saw downstairs, but I was wrong. Gabriel was sitting in the same chair as before, but he had on an orange shirt rather than a green one. His face wore an expression of pain, scrunched and grimacing. He gripped the edge of the desk, his fingers white. The big guy with the snake ink had one mammoth hand on Gabriel's shoulder and was squeezing. The effort didn't show in his face, which was relaxed and smiling. *Click. Click. Click. Click.*

Who the hell was this guy? I was a bit afraid of Dana, but only because she was in a position to hurt my friends, but this guy? I wouldn't want to mess with him. Whatever his name was, I was not going to make fun of it, not even a little bit.

I lowered my camera. Now was probably the time to tell James what I'd found. He may need to look for evidence of who this guy was, and evidence of what role Dana played in all this.

"I have something to show you."

James looked up from the drawer he was perusing. I handed him my camera, took the walkie-talkie out of my pocket, and sat in Gabriel's chair. I may as well have a rest and look at the paperwork James found. Hmm, this receipt was for tea delivered to that café I'd gone to with Patrick, the last person I'd helped arrest. I shuffled through more and found a receipt for Costa. Nooooo! Not my favourite place. Although, again, I should not have been surprised. By the looks of the amount of paper, every place that sold tea had taken delivery of this stuff.

"Thanks, Lily. Yet again, this information is invaluable. I'm going to go down and show Angelica. If anything happens, transport straight home. Got it?"

"Yes, of course. But I thought we'd be okay for now. Wouldn't Gabriel be home not even thinking about this place?"

"You never know. I'll be back." He walked out, leaving

me with tension in my shoulders and sensitivity to any kind of noise. I stood and slid the walkie-talkie back in my pocket. I hadn't checked out the other room, and I didn't know if James had gotten that far. Considering I'd been downstairs for only a short while, it wasn't a shock to find nothing had been touched.

This room had three more filing cabinets, another large desk and office chair, and a water cooler. I went to the first cabinet and opened the bottom drawer. It was filled with suspension files holding manila folders. I leafed through them. More receipts. Holy moly, they were doing big business. But these receipts were from three years ago. Gabriel had obviously been planning for this for a long time.

He'd built his network and hadn't acted until he had maximum exposure. Had he used magic to persuade the retailers to buy his tea? I would imagine he had lots of competition.

I slapped my forehead. Light-bulb moment! Dana could have persuaded shops to take the tea, unless Gabriel had that particular talent, but it wasn't a super common talent, and if he'd been caught, his plan would never have come to fruition. It would be much easier for a PIB agent to get away with something like that.

I skipped the middle drawer, figuring the more recent stuff would be in the top one. I slid it open. It was only a third full. I pulled out the first manila folder. Oh, crap. Things were about to get way worse. There were receipts in here for cafés and supermarkets in London. The tea had been delivered yesterday and the day before. I quickly checked the other folders. There were one hundred and forty businesses we had to confiscate tea from.

I ran downstairs, folders in hand. Angelica and James were standing in the main warehouse, at the beginning of the nearest aisle to the door. They both turned to me when I rushed in. I held the folders up. "We need to hurry. They've delivered the tea to a hundred and forty places in London. The deliveries happened over the last two days."

Angelica's eyes widened, which was the reaction of the century for her. She pressed her lips together. James put one hand on his hip and ran the other hand through his hair.

"Can you bring those here, dear?" Angelica held her hand out. I walked over and gave them to her. She and James leafed through them, James mumbling something, which I assumed was the copy-and-deliver spell he'd mentioned earlier. He didn't exactly call it that, but I needed to name it, and that was nice and obvious, which was necessary if I wanted to remember it existed.

"It's time to clean up and go," Angelica said.

James nodded and turned to me. "Go home, and wait for us. When we get back, we'll have another meeting, but we need to get this cleaned up. Then we have some businesses to visit in London." He looked at Angelica, and she gave a nod.

"Can I help?" It didn't seem fair that they had a whole night's worth of work ahead of them, and I just went home.

"No, dear. We know what to do, and I'm sure James will agree with me when I say I'll be able to concentrate better if I know you're safe at home."

"Okay, then, but if you need me, just walkie-talkie me. Stay safe."

James handed me my camera. "Thanks, Lily. We'll probably be a few hours. It wouldn't hurt to gather some evidence while we're out and about, and I think more interviews are in order tomorrow. I'm going to grab a PIB photo of Dana and show it around, see if she was helping sell the tea. With the magic signatures Angelica's collected tonight, I think we'll have a good case. We can also pull security video from different shops, proving she was involved."

I gave him a quick hug. Feeling as if I was abandoning them, I made my doorway and went home.

Olivia was waiting outside the reception room when I came out. "I'm so glad you're back. I was worried." She looked over my shoulder. "Where are James and Angelica?"

I made a bubble of silence. "They're fine, but they have stuff to clean up. Then they're going somewhere else. We found a trail to all the places selling the tea. They want to find more evidence and interview people. They'll be working all night and into tomorrow. They've just delivered that tea to a lot of places in London."

Her face paled, and she put her hand to her stomach. "Oh my God. I've had some of the tea I bought in London." She stared at me for a moment, her eyes wide. She ran past me and up the stairs. Her thudding footsteps went all the way to the top floor, and then came the slam of a door.

I knew I shouldn't, but I chuckled. The poor thing. I'd have to set her straight, so I trotted upstairs and knocked on her door. I spoke through the closed door. "Liv, there's nothing to worry about. The tea was only delivered yesterday and the day before. It likely hasn't even been unpacked yet, let alone sold. We have all the receipts. I'll ask James where he put them, and we can go through them and check. Okay?"

Her muffled voice came through. "Are you sure?"

"Yes. How long ago did you drink it?"

"Late this afternoon. About five."

"What time is it?" My phone was off and somewhere in the house, so I couldn't check.

"Five past ten."

Was that enough time for it to have taken effect? I'd say it was close but not definitive. "What was the shop called?"

"Tealicious at Leadenhall Hall Market."

"Okay. Just wait there, and I'll contact James and check the receipts. Maybe go to bed. It'll save me from having to transport you there later." I snorted.

"Ha ha, very funny. You know, if I had had the bad tea, I would totally attack you for that comment." I heard the smile in her voice.

"I wouldn't expect anything less. Now, sit tight, and I'll be back."

I magicked James a note. He quickly responded. Apparently, the receipts were in the spare bedroom next to Angelica's. The most recent receipts were in the top box. When I went in there, I found it immediately. There were quite a few boxes lined up next to the bed and two high. I went to the top box nearest the end of the bed. It took me a while to sort through the lot. And then I found it.

Damn! I lowered my head, shut my eyes, and took a deep breath. God, it'd been a long day. I needed sleep, but now I'd have to keep an eye on Olivia. I packed everything away and trudged up the stairs to her room.

"I don't want to worry you, but don't open the door."

"You're kidding."

"I wish I were. The good news is that they only took delivery yesterday afternoon, so chances are that they hadn't stocked the shelves with it." I gently head-butted the door. "I'm so stupid!"

"Why?"

"I could've just gone and checked the actual tea. I'll be back in a sec." Why was I so dumb? I shook my head as I clomped down the stairs. It took me only a few minutes to find and test the tea. I threw my head back and looked at the ceiling. "Thank you, Universe. It's about time you were nice to me."

I hurried back and relayed the good news—her tea was fine.

"Are you sure?"

"Yes, of course I'm sure. Why would I lie about it? I don't have a death wish."

She opened the door slowly. "You could have fooled me when you ran off to find Will."

"Yeah, well...." I shrugged, then let my shoulders fall into a slump. Where was he? Was he okay? Sadness and worry coalesced into a heavy mass that turned my tiredness into exhaustion. "I need to go to bed. I'm done for the day. Angelica and James probably won't be back until tomorrow, but as a precaution, I'd keep that walkie-talkie on. Is that okay if I leave it with you?"

"Of course! Come here." She wrapped her arms around me and squeezed.

"Thanks, Liv. It's just been a long day." I blinked away unwanted tears. "Night."

I showered and got into bed. I snuggled under the covers, trying to chase away the cold that had settled bone deep. We were getting so close to shutting this thing down and catching Dana, but in the meantime, she had free rein to cause as much havoc and heartache as she wanted.

We were nearly there. But if we weren't in time to save Will, it wouldn't be near enough. I lay on my side, stared into the darkness, and tried not to think of never seeing Will again.

A tear escaped and rolled down the side of my face and onto my pillow. The shabbily constructed barriers I used to keep my thoughts away from tragedy were far from water-tight. I wanted that tear to have company in the thousands, but it wasn't time to mourn yet. It was time to fight, and for that, I'd need my wits and strength.

I turned on my other side and closed my eyes. Falling asleep was one of the first battles I'd have to win to get to Will. And if I was anything, it was a fighter.

Dana had started this, but I had to finish it.

Challenge accepted.

CHAPTER 14

The next morning didn't exactly dawn brightly. The satisfying thrum of pelting rain hitting the roof had me wriggling deeper into my covers. I had no idea what time it was because my phone was off and who knew where. Having it near me was not an option. Every time I looked at it, I thought of Dana watching and listening. Having it turned off wasn't good enough. I shuddered.

My jaws opened wide in a yawn. I imagined I might look like a lion roaring, but I probably looked more like a cranky hippopotamus. Staying in bed was more tempting than a bath full of Baci chocolate. Actually, no it wasn't, but since no one was offering me Baci, staying in bed was a good idea. What was there to get up for? When I left this room and went downstairs, I'd be sad and worried because Angelica and James wouldn't be back from averting a

London tea disaster, and then I'd be on edge until they returned.

A flash of light flickered through the narrow gap between the shutters and the edge of my dormer window. "One one thousand, two one thousand." An ear-splitting crack, followed by thunder that could only be described as a hangry giant's tummy rumbling, shook the house. Okay, that might have been an exaggeration. Maybe it was just my brain that shook. That was not the omen I wanted today. I huffed. Argh, what was the use? My brain was definitely awake, and if I stayed here, it would only babble more stupidity.

I threw the covers off and slid out of bed. Today called for grumpy-person lazy clothes. On went the light-grey tracksuit pants, a black long-sleeved T-shirt, and Ugg boots. Yes, I knew it was summer, if barely, but England didn't really know what summer was half the time. Today was definitely one of those times.

I shuffled downstairs and to the kitchen. My coffee had almost finished dispensing when Olivia walked in. "Hey, Lil. How'd you sleep?"

"Took a while to nod off, but once I was there, I owned it. I woke up about fifteen minutes ago." I yawned as proof, which made Olivia yawn. I grinned because it amused me. Lately, things had been stressful and depressing, so I was going to appreciate anything even remotely silly. "I just had a thought. Do you reckon that smiles and yawns are like a virus or something?"

She screwed up her face. "What?"

"Well, they're contagious." I smirked.

"Argh! It's too early for bad jokes. Hurry up and grab your coffee."

My heart did a skippy, racy thing for a few beats. "Do you have news?"

She smiled. "No. It's just, if you're drinking your coffee, you can't talk crap."

I rolled my eyes in fake annoyance. "You obviously have no idea how awesome I am. Excuse me while I go and sit with someone who appreciates my humour." I grabbed my coffee, tossed my head back, and sauntered past her and into the sitting room where an armchair by the fireplace called my name, but not literally.

Olivia followed me in. "I take it you're the one who appreciates you?"

"Yep." I grinned. "But if you want to sit with me, I'll allow it."

She laughed. "You're a nut."

"It's one of my best qualities." I waggled my eyebrows.

Olivia sat in the other chair, and even though the fire-place wasn't lit, it was still cosy to be near it. The atmosphere of another more elegant era permeated from its stone mantle and pretty tiles.

I took a generous sip of my coffee, then hugged the mug to my chest and mumbled the bubble-of-silence spell. I was quite proud of myself for remembering. There was no room for witching badly with Dana out for blood. "Did they call at all?"

"No. The walkie-talkie's been quiet the whole time. You don't think they're in danger, do you?"

"Yes, I do. We're all in danger until Witchface is put away, but I'm pretty confident James and Angelica can handle themselves. I'm worried, but I'm trying not to obsess about it. It won't help." I frowned. There was no way around it: today was going to suck.

"What about Beren? Do you think he's okay?" She worried her bottom lip with her teeth.

"I'm sure he's fine. Out of everyone, he's the safest because Dana has him in her pocket, and he doesn't have as much influence at the PIB now that Angelica's not there. He poses little threat. Hmm, you know… you could call or text him, just ask how he's going. You could just say you hadn't seen him for a while, maybe find out in a super subtle way what's going on at the PIB."

Her gorgeous mass of dark, tightly coiled curls was out today, and she grabbed a section and twirled it around her finger. "I don't know. Won't he be suspicious about why I'm calling?"

"I don't think so. You could always say you're worried about me, that I've been moping about since I was kicked out of the PIB, or you could admit to him that you're totally in love with him and wanted to hear his voice." I snorted.

She grabbed the cushion from her chair and chucked it at me, narrowly missing my head. "Oh, you would have been in big trouble if you'd hit my coffee."

"But I didn't."

"Will you call him? We could do with the extra information. You want to be a police officer and work for the PIB. Why not start practicing the skills you'll need for covert operations?"

"I hardly think I'll be involved in anything like that. I'm more into the research and solving puzzles part of it." She released the curl, and it boinged up, then settled along her neck.

"Pleeease. You know you want to." I gave her my best pleading pouty face.

She rolled her eyes. "Fine, but only because you begged."

Before she called him, there was something I had to do.

"I'm going to put a mind-protection spell on you, so he can't tell what you're really thinking. Normally it would be hard to read a mind from far away, but I want to make sure. He may wonder why, but he can't outright ask you without revealing he's been snooping. Plus, he's not allowed to do that unless it's for an investigation."

"But Beren's a by-the-book kind of guy, isn't he?"

"Yes, and he's one of the nicest people I've ever met, but if he's operating on Dana's implanted agenda...."

"Fair enough."

"It won't hurt. You'll just feel a bit of warmth around your scalp... unless I cut into part of your brain; then you'll know it." I clenched my teeth to keep from laughing. Angelica's morbid sense of humour must be rubbing off on me.

Her face fell, and she shook her head vigorously. "No freaking way! There's no way you're getting near my brain with your magic." She leaned back, away from me.

I snorted. "Just kidding. I'm pretty good at this, and I haven't lobotomised anyone… yet."

"You're not selling this well, Lily. Do you promise not to hurt me?"

"Of course. I'd never suggest it if it were dangerous."

"Okay, but I'm trusting you. Be careful."

"Promise." I mumbled the thought-protection spell. "Done."

Olivia's face relaxed. "Is that it?"

"Yep. I'm going to disappear the silence spell, so from now on, act as if I'm not here, and don't give any information away. If he asks about me, I'm in bed moping, and you have no idea where Angelica is. Don't even mention James."

"Cool. Got it."

I took the bubble of silence away, and she went and grabbed her phone, then returned and settled back in her chair.

She pressed some buttons on her phone and put the phone to her ear. He must have answered because her eyes popped fully open. Her lips parted, but it was a second or two before anything came out. "Ah, hi, Beren. It's Olivia." She turned away from me, probably wanting some kind of privacy, but that was as much as she was going to get.

"Just calling to say hello, also wondered how you were going with all the crime and stuff. I hope you're okay." Gah, how I wished I could hear his side of the conversation. I drummed my fingers on the plush chair arm and my leg bounced up and down.

"Oh, really. Oh, no! That's terrible!"

Oh my God, what was terrible? Talk about torture.

"Is he all right?" She tucked her legs under herself. Getting comfortable, were we? I grinned. It hadn't taken her long to get into the conversation. "Yeah, I've been okay. I'm a bit worried about Lily, though. She said everyone's abandoned her. She just mopes around all day." She tilted her head to the side. "She's in bed. She hasn't been sleeping well—nightmares, I think. So I don't want to bother her. Plus, she's miserable company at the moment." She turned to me and stuck out her tongue. I rolled my eyes so hard that I think I strained a muscle. I did have to give it to her—she was an awesome actress. Maybe she'd missed her calling.

She turned her back to me again and nodded. "Of course. Agreed. So, I was wondering if you'd like to go for coffee or something this week if you're not too busy."

My mouth dropped open. She was so brave. I didn't expect her to go that far in the hopes of getting information. He was likely to say no because he was busy. Then she could get a lead in to ask about work… hopefully.

"Oh, ah, yeah, that's fine. Maybe when your work quietens down. Do you think that will be soon? How's the investigation going? Are you close to catching them? I'm just freaking out because I had an episode, and I don't want it to happen again."

Please, please, please, please, please give her some information we can use. Her voice sounded disappointed when she said, "Oh, okay. That's too bad. Well, let me know if you ever want to take me up on it. Okay. Stay safe. Bye." She pressed the screen on her phone, then set it on the chair next to her. When she turned to me, she was frowning.

I conjured a bubble of silence and stared at her, my eyebrows raised. "Bubble of silence activated. Now, tell me!"

"He turned me down." She sighed.

I pouted to show my sympathy, but we needed to get to the good bits, the information about what was going on at the PIB. "He's not himself—you know that. Plus, you weren't really asking him out. You were fishing for news."

"Well, yes, but still…."

"I hate to be an uncaring witch, and you know your pain is my pain, but what did he say about work?"

"Sheesh, can't a girl have a moment to pick herself up and dust herself off?" She smiled. "I'm okay, and you're right—he's not himself. Also, it's fun keeping you in suspense."

Were we all turning into cruel weirdos who had fun torturing others? I blamed Angelica's influence. "Spill, woman!"

Smirking, she leaned forward. "Well, apparently they're no closer to catching who did it, but they *know* it's related to tea, coffee, scones, and cakes. He thinks they'll be working on it for weeks. He also said Angelica's called in sick again, and so has Drake. He mentioned how well Dana was doing." She rolled her eyes.

I rubbed my forehead with my palm, staving off the headache that threatened. What the hell was Dana doing? Was she putting red herrings in the way? Because I was pretty sure only tea was involved. It wouldn't be hard for her to plant evidence in other foods and beverages since she had a hand in the original crime. "That dirty witch. She's stretching out the investigation as long as she can. This is bad, or it would be if Angelica and James weren't on the case." I shook my head. When we caught her, she was going to spend many, many years in jail. *If* we caught her...

"Thanks for doing that for me. You're awesome. Angelica and James are going to be impressed."

She grinned. "It was kind of fun to see if I could find out anything. I'm looking forward to starting work soon, but I have one stupid exam left, and this week I was supposed to spend studying, but it's kind of gotten away from me."

"Why don't you go study now? There's nothing happening, and since I'm such *miserable company*, it would be a better use of your time." I pulled a silly face at her, and she laughed.

"I might just do that. Let me know when Angelica and James get back. Okay?"

"For sure."

I drained my coffee cup and stared at the fireplace. What was Dana's endgame? She practically had the promotion, so why drag things out? Maybe she was waiting for Drake to die to "solve" the crime? Did she realise things were about to spread to London? I doubted that would make her look good—not stopping it before it went so far. Unless she wanted it to spread? I just couldn't see how she'd benefit from that. Had Gabriel paid her off? That kind of thing was rife in government all over the world. It should be no surprise that crime could affect the PIB too. And her boyfriend did look like the gangster type. Bribery seemed like something he'd be into.

I stood and went to the window. No sign of James or Angelica in the downpour, not that they'd come home that way. Gazing outside was more a habit from growing up. When I'd waited for Dad to get home from work, I'd stand in the lounge room, which was at the front of the house, and stare out the window. Then, after they went missing, I would stand there every night in the first few weeks, just waiting and hoping they'd been found and that they'd be pulling up in a taxi at any moment.

But they never did.

Closing my tear-filled eyes, I tried to recall the last time I'd seen them. After big squishy hugs for me, and not so squishy ones for James, they'd walked outside to the red-and-white taxi. Dad had held the car door open for Mum as the taxi driver put their suitcases in the boot.

James and I had stood in the doorway, Mum's friend behind us. Dad had turned and waved, a huge smile on his face, then got in the taxi. I'd missed them even before the taxi was out of sight. If only Mum had used her clairvoyance, she could have saved us all a lot of heartache. Unless she had and didn't tell anyone. Maybe whatever they went through in England was the lesser of two evils. A wave of nausea coasted through my stomach.

I opened my eyes. If them disappearing was the better option, I hated to think what the worse one was.

Argh, this line of thinking wouldn't help anyone. It might be hours before James and Angelica returned.

Time would drag on more torturously than being drawn and quartered if I didn't do something to distract myself. I sat back in the armchair, and my iPad popped into my hands. This magic gig had its uses. A light and fluffy romance was just what I needed. At least someone was getting some action, even if it was just a character in a book.

LATER IN THE AFTERNOON, OLIVIA AND I WERE SITTING AT the kitchen table matching wits at chess—okay, so I may have put a positive spin on the situation. Her wits actually had mine on the ground in a headlock, and mine were turning blue.

"Checkmate." She sat back in her chair and folded her arms, a grin on her face.

"Like it's a surprise. I don't know why you bother playing with me. It's not like I'm any competition."

She shrugged. "You'll improve if we keep playing. Plus, studying was doing my head in. I needed a break to relax my brain."

"Ha ha. Because there's no thinking needed when you play me." I snorted.

"I have to have something I'm better at. You get to be a witch."

"True, but it's not all fun. Before I got my powers, I'd never had my life threatened, not even once. It's getting old, fast."

"Would you give back your powers if you could trade it for being safe and living a normal life?"

I put my elbow on the table and rested my chin in my palm. "I don't know. Maybe yes. I would miss certain aspects of it, of course, but I can't remember the last time I had a proper night's sleep or went out without worrying someone was going to kill me." I sighed. "Anyway, it is what it is. Sorry for seeming ungrateful." I mumbled the bubble of silence spell. "I'm just tired and worried about Will and Beren. Plus, even if we can prove who perpetrated this violence thing, how are we going to put Dana in jail if she has most of the agents in the PIB under her control? It's the whole of the PIB versus three of us. I don't really like those odds."

Footsteps sounded from the hallway. Then Angelica appeared at the door, James and someone else behind her. "Hello, dears. Mind if we join you?" Dark circles had embedded under her eyes, but from her smile and the person next to James, I'd say our odds just improved. To say I was surprised would be an understatement.

I altered the bubble of silence to include everyone.

Angelica stepped into the room and gestured to our guest. "Olivia, you remember Agent Drake Pembleton, my boss at the PIB?"

I never thought I'd ever be happy to see Drake, but the world was a funny place.

"Hello, Agent Pembleton." Olivia stood and held her hand out. He came in and shook it.

Drake turned to me and cleared his throat. He

smoothed down his tie in a nervous gesture that I remembered only too well. His face was drawn—he'd lost weight since I'd seen him last—and he had similar dark circles to Angelica's. Probably a result of Dana's "virus."

"Hello, Lily. I'm afraid I owe you an apology."

Two surprises in one day, and I didn't even like surprises, but I'd make an exception for these. I wasn't ready to answer him yet, though. He'd need to expand on the apology sentiment. I'd been through hell in the last week. It was only fair someone else joined me. And it wasn't as if he'd always been nice to me, even without Dana's influence.

He swallowed and licked his bottom lip. "I realise we… I treated you unfairly. I never would have banished you if Dana hadn't put the thought into my head. I'm embarrassed this has happened, and I promise you, once I'm reinstated, you have the PIB's full support."

I nodded. "Okay, thanks." I gave him that closed-mouth, just-slightly-more-curved-than-straight smile, the one you gave when you didn't really want to smile, but you had to be polite. If he still felt a bit awkward because I wasn't overjoyed, bad luck. It wasn't my job to make people feel better when they'd treated me unfairly numerous times. Maybe he'd think twice before he disrespected me next time, because I had no doubt this newfound niceness wouldn't last more than a few weeks.

Now that was out of the way, I stood and gave my brother a ginormous hug.

"What's that for?" he asked, knowing I wasn't generally a hugger.

I stood back. "I was worried about you."

He smiled. "I can take care of myself."

"I know. It's just that Dana has a lot of resources at her command, and she would clearly do anything to get her way. If she found out what you were doing, she'd probably kill you. At the very least, she'd have you arrested for some trumped-up charge. So how did today go?"

"We stopped all the deliveries from getting to the shelves. We've confiscated the lot, and it's in a secure storage facility. We've also got sworn interviews and video evidence of Dana's involvement. Then, after that, we went and helped Mr Pembleton." James nodded at Drake.

Drake rubbed the back of his head. "Thanks again, Agent Bianchi. You and Agent DuPree showed up just in time."

I looked at Angelica. "So, what's our plan now, Ma'am?"

Her smile was demure. "We're going to disavow Dana of the notion that she runs the PIB. I believe you younger folk would refer to it as 'taking her down.'"

I grinned. Karma was a witch with a bun, impeccable dress sense, and a gruesome sense of humour.

And she was ready to rumble.

CHAPTER 15

T he next morning, we were all up and ready to go by nine. Angelica and James had been so busy the day before that they needed to recuperate so they'd be strong enough to deal with Dana. Drake needed time to heal as well. We were sitting around the kitchen table in our PIB suits—even I'd donned one today. Angelica said it was important that we presented a united front. Plus, it would piss off Dana, and the angrier she was, the more likely she'd be to make a mistake.

I bit my nails, and my leg bounced under the table like a hyperactive squirrel on a pogo stick. I was pretty sure my resting heart rate was 150 beats per minute. Today was going to be dangerous, and we still didn't know where Will was, or even if he was still alive. I swallowed and bit the inside of my cheek. I was not going to cry.

A radio receiver sat on the table. James had recruited

one of his army contacts who was also a witch. He was going to help coordinate everything from here with Olivia's help. We each had a walkie-talkie so we could keep Sergeant Crawford and Olivia updated. That way, we could all be accounted for if things went south.

A two-person-sized cage with thick magic-infused steel bars stood in the corner. It was for Gabriel. Stage one of Operation Piranha Fishing—I know; I couldn't believe they agreed to my suggestion either—was to arrest Gabriel, then get him out of harm's way and secure the warehouse. He would be able to testify against Dana in court, so we needed him alive and coherent.

The next job was to lure Dana out on her own. If she saw us coming, she would bring a whole army of PIB Agents, and that would create a disaster we couldn't afford, not to mention it would be noticed by a lot of people— witch wars were hardly subtle.

For this part, I would take my phone and show up at the warehouse after Gabriel had been arrested. As soon as Dana knew I was out and about, she would come for me. I wasn't too arrogant to admit I was scared witchless.

Whatever happened from there was something we couldn't plan for. James would read her mind to find Will, and we would have to remove the ring if we wanted everyone else's zombified state reversed. Once everyone had their right minds back, things would be fine. But until then, there was no way we'd be able to catch Dana and put her in jail.

Drake nodded at Angelica. She stood, her face grim.

"Unfortunately, this is not the first civil war we've had at the PIB. Although the last one was over twenty years ago, it feels as fresh as yesterday to me. Eleven agents died that day."

Oh, crap. I'd never heard about that. All the moisture drained from my mouth and throat, and I coughed. We really were going to war.

She continued, "Everyone knows what they're to do. I know you're not trained for this, Lily, but you must show no mercy. If it's one of our lives or Dana's or her agents, you must kill."

Her gaze bored into mine, her unspoken words like a knife poised to slice my heart—if Will or her own nephew, Beren, tried to hurt us, we had to kill them. I wasn't sure I could. In fact, I knew I couldn't.

She raised a brow, her stare turning to granite. "If you can't do this, Lily, you'll have to stay here. I can't afford any mistakes."

We would just have to neutralise Dana before any of that happened. I would die trying rather than kill my friends. It would have to be good enough. I took a deep breath and made my voice steady, determined. "I'll die before I let her win." She gave me a nod. Whether she saw the cop-out in my words, I didn't know.

"Ready?" She looked at James, then Drake. They nodded and stood. They each made their own doorway and stepped through. I was waiting here, out of the way, until they returned with Gabriel—we obviously didn't want Piranha there early.

I bit the nails on my right hand. Then I swapped to the

left. Olivia's gaze sailed around the room, and Sergeant Crawford sat and watched the radio transmitter.

Waiting sucked.

God, now I needed to go to the toilet. I'd only been about twenty minutes ago, so I knew I didn't really need to, but my damn nerves were freaking out. I shifted from one bum cheek to the other. No way was I going. Angelica could be back any second, and I'd have to grab my phone and move—I'd left it on in the sitting room so it didn't look suspicious when I suddenly turned it on later, and because of the bubble of silence we had in the kitchen, Dana wouldn't have been able to listen in.

Disembodied muffled voices floated in the air before a dishevelled-looking Gabriel stumbled through a doorway, James shoving him from behind. Special magic-blocking PIB handcuffs secured the red-haired criminal's hands behind his back.

Gabriel scowled and tried to jerk out of James's grip. James dragged him to the cage. The door automatically swung open. James shoved the cuffed witch in and shut the door, which clanged loudly and was momentarily outlined by a golden glow.

I narrowed my eyes at the prisoner, anger sizzling beneath the surface, warming my blood. He'd caused so much pain. Selfish bastard. There was so much I wanted to say to him.

But he beat me to it. "What are you starin' at, stupid witch? You think you're all high and mighty, locking me up. But you're the ones who 'ave it wrong. They'll kill all of us, given a chance. Just you watch. Keep 'em in disarray, and we'll 'ave the upper 'and." He sneered at me. "Fools. Non-witches are little more than animals. The sooner you realise that, the better off we'll all be." He gripped the bars. Electric-blue sparks showered from where he touched the cage. The magic barrier hissed and crackled. Gabriel screamed, jerked his hands back, and blew on them. "Bastards."

I shook my head. Bad luck, buddy. As much as I wanted to tell him how much he deserved that and more, I kept my mouth shut. Arguing with him would be pointless and would only rile me up further. I had bigger fish to fry—a piranha, in fact.

James folded his arms. "Oh, yeah, don't touch the bars. You'll get zapped."

Gabriel gave James a death stare and growled.

James turned towards me and lifted his chin in a let's-get-going gesture. I ran into the sitting room and grabbed my phone. Before I stepped through my doorway, I created a return-to-sender spell—who knew what I'd be walking into. I took a deep breath. *Here goes nothing.*

I appeared in the alleyway and crept to where it opened into the car park. I stuck my head around the corner. No one was around. I wondered if Angelica had something to do with that. Someone tapped me on the shoulder. I let out a brief scream before slamming my hand over my mouth and turning. James stood there, his eyes wide.

I angrily whispered, "Well, what did you expect? That was stupid. Don't sneak up on me."

A smile threatened to break out, but he wisely kept it in check. "Sorry."

"You could have blown our cover."

"Don't worry. We've made sure everyone's staying inside today."

I would have asked how, but we didn't have time. Dana was probably already on her way. I jogged to the driveway, turned left, and ran all the way to Gabriel's building.

The pedestrian door was shut, but the roller door was open. We walked into the main warehouse area where Angelica and Drake waited. Angelica spoke into her walkie-talkie, probably confirming we were all at the warehouse and ready to go. Having the large door open gave me the creeps, but we didn't want Dana suspecting something untoward was going on. For all she knew, I was spying.

Drake turned to me, his expression reserved and serious. "Remember, Lily, do whatever you can to protect yourself, and let us worry about grabbing her ring. We want you to get out of this safely."

"Thank you. I appreciate it. I'll do my best." I forced my tense face into a smile. He was actually being decent and seemed as if he meant it.

"Time to spread out." James drew his gun. "Lily, you go to the back of the warehouse. If she wants to get to you, she has to come through us."

We'd already discussed this, and I didn't like it. I wanted to fight my own battles. She was stronger than me, but I wasn't helpless, and to put Angelica and James in danger went against the grain, even though they were trained professionals. I was probably crazy, but what else was new?

Plus, Dana was scared of me. I didn't know why, but she was; otherwise, why go to this extent to get me out of her way? But I did as I was told. This was no time to believe I knew better. They'd done this many times before. I had no idea, and I'm sure once things started, it would be all I could do to keep myself alive.

We expected her to turn up by herself, but what if she didn't?

I reached the shelves that ran across the back of the warehouse and turned to face the door. James and Angelica stood against opposite walls about halfway along, and Drake stood in the middle, between them.

Anticipation and fear coiled within me, tightening my shoulders and clamping my jaw shut. I stared at the large opening and car park beyond. My hands clenched and unclenched, and my ears strained for any indication she'd arrived. What if she had coordinates for inside the building? Surely Angelica and James had thought of that. Maybe they'd set an alarm upstairs. If she was going to pop in somewhere, I wouldn't imagine she would pop into the warehouse zone where she could get hit by a forklift.

Warm tingles traced up and down my nape. I shuddered.

She was here.

Oh, correction: *they* were here.

Crap.

Dana stood at the front of maybe fourteen agents, who

fanned out, covering the whole front opening of the building. William stood next to her. My stomach did a little flip, happy he was alive.

His gaze found mine, cool and aloof. If there had once been any affection or attraction, it was smothered, buried deep under Dana's darkness. William was ready to do whatever she asked. I should celebrate that she hadn't killed him, but my heart shrank from his dispassionate observation. If we weren't in such a precarious position, I would have slunk into a corner to lick my wounds.

Dana regarded Will, then smirked at me. Stupid witch. I narrowed my eyes and glared at her. She shouldn't mistake my heartache for weakness. I was ready to do what I had to. Whatever the cost.

Then her eyes flicked to Drake, and her confidence wavered for an instant. Surprise! I bet she hadn't expected to see him up and running around. But she quickly recovered and put her hands on her hips, offering him a saccharine smile. "Hello, sir. I'm so happy to see you've recovered."

She started to walk towards him, probably hoping to reinstate her spell, but Angelica said, "Stop right there, Agent Lam."

I couldn't help it; I swear. I bleated. Loudly.

Dana halted and turned her furious gaze on me. At least I'd distracted her from whatever crazy plan she had. Keep 'em off balance was my new motto. If you couldn't beat them with experience, confuse them with randomness.

She took another step.

James approached her. She stopped and turned her head

to watch him. She held her arm out straight, and a gun appeared in her hand. "Come any closer, Agent Bianchi, and I will shoot you." Hmm, way to get around a return-to-sender spell, and I would bet my most-comfortable pair of underwear that everyone else was packing. Being a civilian really sucked sometimes.

He halted and pointed his gun at her. "Wanna see who's faster?" Hmm, snark must run in the family. Genetics rocked.

She didn't take her eyes off James when she said, "Beren, William, you know what to do. All these people are under arrest for trespassing. They're also charged with treason, which carries a maximum penalty of life in a PIB prison." She grinned, her teeth looking very piranha-ie. "That's if they don't resist arrest, and we have to shoot them."

Beren, his footsteps measured and robot-like, approached his aunt. I knew Angelica's orders to kill included herself, if it came to that. Was she regretting that stance right now? Her poker face was engaged, so it was hard to tell.

William moved towards me, stony-faced, devoid of emotion. A cold wind blew through the chambers of my heart, buffeting the flame I'd been carrying for him. My breathing came faster. He had almost reached me. Was he going to hurt me or cuff me and throw me in a PIB cell?

"Not so smart now, are you, petal?" Dana cackled like the witch she was.

But I didn't spare her anymore thought. The man I'd

thought I was falling in love with had stopped in front of me. His blue-grey eyes regarded me dispassionately. Normally intense and full of heat—even if it was because of crankiness some of the time—they were the dull battleship grey of a scuttled warship. If I tapped on his heart, I bet it would echo its emptiness.

Movement registered near the doors as the agents swarmed in and surrounded Angelica, James, and Drake. But I couldn't think of that now. All I could do was try to breathe and will my heart to keep beating, even as it was torn apart.

William held out handcuffs. "Lily Bianchi, you're under arrest for trespassing and treason. Turn around and put your hands on the shelf behind you."

"Will? It's me. I'm your friend."

He didn't flinch. Nothing changed. "Please turn around, Miss Bianchi, or I'll be forced to do it for you."

"If she resists, Will, darling, you have my permission to kill her." Dana just couldn't help herself. I took a deep breath, letting the fury seep in and spread through me. No way would she get away with this.

This could be the last move I ever made, but if I didn't try, we were all going to jail for the rest of our lives, and that was if Dana didn't come up with an excuse to shoot us all.

I engaged my third eye, reached out my hand, and grabbed Will's wrist. "It's me, Will. Lily. You don't want to arrest me. I know you don't." I saw his golden aura, but it was intertwined with grey ribbons that dulled its lustre. Whether that was Dana or the ring she wore, I didn't know.

He reached out his other hand and grabbed my other arm. Just as he went to spin me around and cuff me, I used the energy inside me to reach out and touch the warmth that emanated from his aura. I channelled my feelings into it —the affection, the attraction, the respect, and, yes, even the love that was a mere bud but had potential to grow. I threw in memories, of him staring at me in the rear-view mirror, of him grinning at a quip I'd made, of our time training in James's shed.

My desperate heart was full to bursting, the emotions I'd conjured pulling me into a vortex of sensations. In the maelstrom, I was sure I'd felt the feather-light touch of the real him. I tried to hold it, draw it into me and out of Dana's shackles—his intensity and passion. The person he was. Sweat dampened my face, and it was as if I had a fever.

His grip on my arm squeezed tighter. He clenched his jaw and shut his eyes, as if he were trying to resist. Fear, frustration, and anger pulsed through the bond.

But he didn't come back, didn't open his eyes and tell me everything was going to be okay.

Tears burnt my eyes. It wasn't working. My idea was as stupid as I was, which made total sense. I didn't want to give up, but I couldn't kill him. I held onto the power and my link to him, just in case it was doing something—however small—hung my head and started to turn towards the shelves.

William swayed and used me for support. I released his wrist and tried to spin around in time to put my free hand out and stop myself from smashing into the shelves, but I wasn't quick enough.

My chest slammed into a shelf, William's weight crushing me from behind. Pain lanced from my sternum into my back. I couldn't breathe. I dropped my link to the magic river, severing my connection to Will. It was as if someone had punched me in the stomach. Sorrow washed in, drowning me.

If I made a doorway around myself, I could escape, but then I'd pretty much cut William in half. There was no use trying an attack spell because he had a return-to-sender spell on.

More than one person shouted. Scuffling, a grunt. Someone else—James?—screamed, "No!"

A gun went off, the sound ricocheting through the space.

It was as if a kebab stick had skewered my eardrums. I shut my eyes. My whole world had been reduced to ringing ears and the inability to breathe because of the pain and Will's weight. I wanted to fight, but I found myself thinking, *just cuff me already*. What was taking him so long? Had he been shot? My mouth went dry. He wasn't moving, but nor had he fallen. I needed to breathe. I wanted to scream for help, but only a squeak came out.

"Now take them away." Dana's voice came from behind Will.

I tried to shout, "no," but nothing happened. A tear leaked from the corner of my eye. This could not be happening.

Then there was warm breath at my ear. I could only just

hear over the ringing. "Lily, it's Will. I'm here. You brought me back." He turned me towards him. When he stared into my eyes, the deadness was gone. It was him! I grinned despite the fiery agony in my sternum. Happy warmth spread through me, banishing the despair. "Wait here."

Will turned and ran towards Dana, who had her back to him, obviously not anticipating any threat. A small axe appeared in his hand. My mouth dropped open. Oh my God, he wasn't going to—

Close to her, he grabbed the hand with the ring. Before she could react, he pulled her to the ground, slapping her hand flat against the concrete. He raised his arm, and then swept the axe down.

Dana's shriek was even more ear-piercing than the gunshot. I covered my ears as she continued screaming. I put my hand on my breastbone for support, ready to run if Will needed me. He would surely get pounded from all the agents, but they stood dazed. Many were blinking, shaking their heads, turning to one another with questioning looks on their faces.

Holy crap! Will had done it! I tentatively stepped forward and gazed around, trying to find James in the confusion. Had they already taken him to jail? Was he okay? Angelica was gone too, but Drake was on the floor, face down, still, blood pooling under him and spreading slowly across the concrete.

My breath caught in my throat. As much as he wasn't my favourite person, my first thought was, poor man. My second thought, which made me feel guilty as hell, was,

thank God it wasn't James, Angelica or Beren. My third
thought while I was backing away in horror was, shame it
wasn't Piranha.

I looked up. William dragged her to her feet. Her cheeks
glistened with tears. She held her arm to her chest, her
other arm protecting it. There was no blood, so I had to
assume Will had done something to the blade, like made it
hot enough to cauterize the wound, or maybe he just
magicked it shut?

Could today get any more gruesome? Will's arm hung
by his side, and he held Dana's dismembered hand. "Ew."

He gestured to two agents. "Take her to the PIB and
process her. Then lock her up." Two men grabbed one
arm each.

Dana snarled. "You can't arrest me! I'm the PIB's best
agent. You've ruined everything. What's wrong with you? I
always knew you were an idiot, but I never realised how
much of one you were. You useless, pathetic nothing. No
wonder you could never be the man I needed." She spat at
him, as in germy phlegm. Wow, that was attractive.

"Give it up, Dana. It's over." Will shook his head.

Her eyes shone with psychopathic glitter. "It's not over,
Will. It won't be over until we win. We're just getting
started. And don't you think you'll get away with this."
She tried to raise her stump, but one agent held her
arm down.

She swivelled her head to look at him and growled.
Then she looked at Will. "I'll be back, and when I am, I'll
kill you all!" She turned her head and eyeballed the eight

agents that remained. One or two shrank back, another shook her head, and the others smirked.

She really had lost the plot.

I felt the slimy touch of familiar magic. "Will, no one's handcuffed her!"

Dana's mouth opened wide, revealing her glistening teeth, and she cackled. Then she stared straight at me. "Until we meet again, petal. You can't escape your destiny with us." Anger twisted her features as she stepped towards me.

Will jumped between us, and I gritted my teeth, ready to stand my ground.

And then she disappeared.

"What the—?" I looked around Will. She really was gone, and so was the dirty magic. I had no idea if that's what it was called, but it felt that way to me. My legs shook like jelly as I considered what her disappearing meant.

We'd failed.

She'd won.

I'd forever be watching out for her until she showed up again, and I had no doubt she would.

Everyone's heads turned this way and that.

I grabbed my scalp. "How could you let her get away? Why wasn't she cuffed?" The handcuffs would have prevented her from accessing magic. My throat burned, and I forced myself not to cry.

The shorter agent with the buzz cut, who'd been holding her, said, "I'm sorry, Agent Blakesley. I was going to, but she only had a stump. The cuffs would have fallen off."

Will growled. "They would've worked even if they were only on one wrist." He looked to the ceiling. After a few deep breaths, he addressed the remaining agents. "I want this place cordoned off. It's a crime scene. I'm going to send forensics and someone to photograph and collect Agent Pembleton's body."

He turned around and stared at Drake's sprawled form, and then at me, the fight in his gaze fading. He stepped closer and gave me a tentative smile. His voice was gentle when he said, "Hey."

"Hey."

"This is probably a stupid question and too early, but are we okay? I can't remember everything that happened while I was under her control, but I'm sorry. I do remember today, and that day you were kicked out of the PIB. I know I've helped put you through hell. I don't expect you to forgive me right now, but I hope you'll be able to one day, same as I hope I can forgive myself." He swallowed, his Adam's apple bobbing with the effort.

"It wasn't your fault." I shook my head. "You two have history, and she had that ring." I screwed up my face and kept from looking down at the severed appendage. Why was he still holding it?

"Before she spelled me, I was pretending to be okay with her. I would never trust her in a million years. Something seemed off about her, and I wanted to get to the bottom of it. Her showing up out of the blue—well, it's not like her. She plans everything—always has. She never does anything without a good reason. When she arrived, she said she'd missed me and London." He rolled his eyes. "I'm sorry I couldn't tell you then, but I didn't want to put you on her radar. It was hard keeping it from you. And if she'd known we were friends, you would have been even more of a target... at least, that's what I thought. She seems to have a particularly violent hatred of you. I tried to keep the fact that I cared about you a secret. But I obviously didn't do a very good job." He tilted his head to the side, his eyes boring into mine with the sexy intensity I remembered.

The last bit of my resolve to hold a bit of anger disappeared. Will had been who I'd thought all along, but then Dana turned everything to crap. "Well, she obviously wanted to run the PIB. I doubt she would have admitted that."

"I sense there's more to it. And you heard what she said when she left. Do you have any idea what that's about?"

"No. I have no idea." I braced myself and looked at the five-fingered lump in his hand. "Can we maybe stow that at the PIB and check on James and Angelica?"

He looked at Dana's hand, and he started, as if he'd forgotten it was there. O... kay.

I made my door first and stepped through. Will arrived a split second after me and hurried to beat me to the reception-room door. He pressed the intercom. "I want to make sure everyone knows you're with me. I don't want anything happening to you, Lily." The look he gave me was sincere and full of emotion. My heart was a gooey, melted-chocolate mess. Sappy, I know, but I'd been waiting for this for a long time. He was cute, even holding a severed hand.

A female agent wearing an earpiece opened the door. He took her aside, far enough away that I couldn't hear, and they had a quick discussion. He returned to me, relief relaxing his face. "Angelica and James are fine. They're in the boardroom, trying to sort everyone out. When Dana's link to the ring was broken, everyone was pretty much in shock and had no idea what they were supposed to be doing. James has been asking about you, though."

"Well, let's not keep him waiting."

We hurried along the hallway, stabbing pains in my sternum making me breathe faster and shallower. We still reached the boardroom in record time. Will knocked but didn't wait for an answer before he opened the door. James was sitting in his regular spot next to Angelica. He did a double take when he saw me. He jumped to his feet, ran over and threw his arms around me. I grunted at the shooting pain in my chest.

"Are you hurt?" He leaned back.

"I think so. It might just be cartilage. I got a bit squashed against the shelves."

"Why didn't you tell me you were hurt, Lily?" Will stared at me, his brow wrinkled in such a familiar pattern.

I placed my palm on my sternum and shrugged. Oops, shouldn't have done that. I grimaced. "I wouldn't worry about this. But could someone please take that hand away?" I cocked my head towards Will's side.

He lifted the hand. "Oh, this old thing? Oops, I forgot."

"Ew, man. You got Dana's hand? You could've bagged it, for God's sake. Dude!" James wrinkled his nose, and a plastic evidence bag appeared in his hand. He held it open, and Will dropped it in. "I'll take this to evidence. Be back soon. And wash your hands, you grub." He hurried out.

Will mumbled something, and his hands were clean again.

Angelica spoke from her spot just to the left of the head of the table. She'd left that seat vacant, probably for Drake. I hung my head and let a small wash of sadness lap against me. He'd been there to help at the end. He hadn't been the bad guy after all. "We've transferred Gabriel to a cell. He's going to stay there until the trial in six weeks. Where's Agent Pembleton? And is Dana in the cells?"

My attention had been well and truly occupied when the shot rang out. Angelica and James must have been brought here just as that went down. I looked up at Will, my face solemn. "I think you should explain everything."

He nodded, and we approached the table. Four agents I didn't know were there, but Beren wasn't. "Is Beren okay?"

Angelica nodded, her mouth slightly open. "Yes, thank God. I've sent him through the building to take stock of what we're dealing with now that Dana's not in charge. So, where is she?"

Will pulled a seat out for me, and I sat. Hmm, this was a nice change, and so was the lack of I-hate-you-and-wish-you-would-die vibes coming from around the table. I was totally going to enjoy my new Dana-free existence.

Except she could pop back at any moment. My heart palpitated, and I gripped my chair arms.

"Are you all right, Lily?" Will had sat next to me, and his face showed genuine concern.

"I'll be okay. Maybe just tell Angelica everything. Then can we find Beren and get me healed?"

"Of course." He smiled, then turned to Angelica. "You're not going to like this. We stuffed up. She got away." He bravely held her gaze.

She paused, maybe digesting the information? I tensed, waiting for her outburst, but it never came. "We all failed today, William. I did have a backup plan in case we were arrested, and it didn't actually come to that, but I underestimated her, which meant we had to go along with what she wanted. We're going to have to overhaul protocols. We'll be studying that ring—we need to come up with protections to make sure nothing like this can ever happen again. We've been complacent too long. Dealing with petty criminals is one thing, but this is altogether something different." She clasped her hands on the table in front of her and stared at them for a moment. When she looked up, I could see pain in her eyes. "Thank you, Will. He wasn't always my greatest supporter, but he was a loyal agent who gave everything he had to this organisation." She stood. "Excuse me."

She left the room and shut the door behind her. "How did she know?" I asked him.

"I took down my mind shield."

"Oh." I guessed that was easier than having to say the words. Oh, crap! Olivia was probably waiting for news. I felt in my pocket for my phone. It was still there, miracle of miracles. I took it out and dialled Olivia.

"Lily! Oh my God, it's so good to hear your voice! Are you okay? Angelica checked in a few minutes ago, but she didn't know where you were. I've been so worried."

"I'm okay. Piranha got away though, but Will chopped off her hand, so that's something."

"Oh. That's… hmm. So, you got the ring?"

"Yes. It's gone down to evidence. There's more to tell, but I don't have time right now." My chest throbbed. That would teach me for taking a proper breath. "I have a small injury. I'm just off to have Beren heal me."

"Is he back to normal?"

"I haven't seen him yet, but I believe so. Will is too." I smiled.

"That's wonderful news. Look, I'll let you go, but come straight home afterwards."

"Of course. Where else would I go?"

She giggled. I glanced at Will and blushed. He raised his eyebrows in question.

"Um, I don't think so, Liv. I'll see you later. And thanks for today."

"I'm always here for you. See you soon."

"Are you ready to find Beren?" Will asked.

"Yes, thanks. If I don't get this fixed, I won't be able to sleep."

He placed his hand over mine. "I'm so sorry, Lily."

I looked over at the other agents, strangers, who were watching all this with bated breath. Bunch of gossipy pervs. "Let's go." I stood and led the way to the door.

We tracked Beren down to the front desk where he was

looking over paperwork. When he looked up and met my eyes, I knew the old Beren was back. I grinned. "Hey, person who was a stranger and is now my friend again."

"Shit. I'm so sorry, Lily. You have to know I never would have abandoned you if I was in my right mind. I could kill myself for the way I treated you. And I can't believe we let Dana come after you." He shook his head and ran a hand through his blonde hair. "I know I have no right to ask you this, but are we okay?"

I shared a smile with Will—it was the same question he'd asked me not twenty minutes ago. "Yep. We're all good. Just don't let it happen again." I gave him a half smile.

He came in for a hug, but I held my hand up. "Um, no hugs. I'm a bit broken. It happened in the drama at the warehouse." I pointed to my sternum. "I'm not sure, but it might be cracked or strained or something. I have no idea, but it hurts."

"Come with me." Will and I followed Beren to a small, white room that had a vacant desk and two chairs. Once we were all inside, he shut the door. "Sit." He pointed to the chair.

I sat. He pulled up the other chair and sat opposite me, our knees touching. "Where does it hurt?"

I placed my hand in the middle of my chest.

"Okay. I'll put my hand on your shoulder. You might feel a moment of pain. Ready?"

"Yes."

Will knelt next to my chair, held out his hand, and gave me a questioning look. I blinked back tears and nodded, then placed my hand in his. He squeezed it and gave me a reassuring smile.

I shut my eyes. Beren placed his hand on my shoulder and got to work. Heat radiated down my arm and through the bones in my chest. Pinching caused me to gasp, but it didn't last long. The warmth travelled from the middle of my chest to the back of my ribs. Then it was over. Beren removed his hand, and I opened my eyes.

"How does it feel?" Beren's gaze was assessing.

I twisted one way, then the other, took a deep breath. "Fantastic. No pain. Thank you, B." I stood and gave him a hug. His arms came around me, gentle and familiar. We would all heal and get past this. Dana's evil wasn't enough to destroy us. That made me smile.

Will tapped me on the shoulder. "Mind if I cut in?"

Beren grinned. "Yeah, I could do with another hug." He released me and held his arms wide for Will. I snorted. Ah, these were the guys I remembered. They both laughed.

Beren clapped Will on the shoulder. "I know when I'm not wanted." He winked. "But don't be too long. Just before you found me, I got a message that Angelica's calling an emergency meeting that starts in"—he looked at his watch —"ten minutes. Behave, you two." He waggled his brows and shut the door.

Will gazed down at me with a fierceness I recognised only too well. Seemed like the body was happy to jump in before the brain was ready. "Can I give you a hug?"

I nodded. He slid his hands around my waist, and I snuggled into his chest, just breathing in his familiar scent.

Before I could stop it, my mouth said, "I've missed you." Stupid mouth, giving everything away too soon. We'd only just reconciled like thirty minutes ago. I knew it hadn't been his fault, but I couldn't erase the weeks I'd felt abandoned by him and rejected.

He kissed the top of my head. I froze at the unexpected affection. He really did like me. "I know it might take some time for us to fix things, but I promise if you can learn to trust me again, I'll make it worth your while."

I smiled but kept my cheek pressed against his warm chest. "Yeah. How so?"

"I'll supply you with endless cappuccinos and double-chocolate muffins. I promise to go running with you whenever you want and not trail behind. I also promise to always have your back. From now on, you'll always know where you stand with me. I'm so sorry." He rubbed circles on my back.

As much as I didn't want this to end—God knew I'd spent long enough waiting to be in his arms—we had to be at this meeting soon. I gently pushed back to look up into his eyes, my hands settling on his waist. "Thanks. It's going to take some time for me, though. I've been through a lot these last few weeks." A tear escaped and trickled down my cheek. I'd have to have a word with that renegade tear duct later. I hadn't given it permission to make me look as sad as I felt. "I know this is probably TMI, but you broke my heart. I know we weren't dating, but I thought there was something there. Maybe I read too much into it…." I looked down. I never wanted to put myself in that position again. I needed to get it out, and he could do what he liked with the information. If he didn't feel anything stronger than friendship for me, it was best I knew it now. Then I really could work on moving on and leaving these feelings behind. "I was hoping we'd date, Will, but if that's not a direction you can see us going in, I'd like you to be honest with me. And none of this is your problem. I'll be cool with being friends. It just may take me a while to adjust."

Sadness swept through his eyes. He lifted his hand and ran the back of it down my cheek. The hibernating butterflies all shocked into flight at once. I was a goner. Dammit. "I'm sorry I hurt you. I wasn't trying to."

I smiled. "I know. It's my own stupid brain misinterpreting things."

He shook his head. "You didn't misinterpret anything, Lily. You do drive me crazy, but generally, it's a good kind of crazy. I wasn't lying when I told you I didn't want to get into a relationship with anyone, but as much as I've tried to talk myself out of us, I've run out of reasons. Dana hurt me, but that is truly in the past. I can't live in the shadows of pain I should've discarded ages ago. We only get one life, and I want to explore us. But I know you need time, and to be honest, I do too. These last few weeks have been trying for both of us, but if you think you can trust me again, I'd like to try." He smiled, his dimples doing stupid, irresistibly dimply things.

"I'd like to trust you, and I'm down with giving us a go too, but taking it slowly would be a great idea." Okay, this was my brain talking. My libido had other ideas, but it wasn't in charge… at least not this time.

"So, I'm thinking we should start with a morning run on Saturday. It's a long way to a dinner date from there, so we'll both be safe."

"Okay. I would love to."

If anyone had walked in on us, they would have rolled their eyes and gagged: we were staring at each other with goofy grins like a couple of teenagers who'd never dated anyone before. We were adults, for goodness' sake. But it felt wonderful to be happy, as if my chest was going to burst from being filled with all the good things.

He tapped my nose, his gaze travelling to my mouth. The room was so quiet. Could he hear how loudly I was breathing? Was I ready to kiss him? Was he even thinking of kissing me? Gah! I wanted out of my head. It was hell in here.

My phone rang, and I jumped. He dropped his arms, and I reached into my back pocket to grab it. "Hello?"

"Lily, we're waiting for you and William. Please hurry it along." Angelica sounded two parts stern, one part amused. I blushed.

"Ah, yes, Ma'am. We'll be right there."

I hung up. Will grinned. "Shall we?" He opened the door and followed me through. On the way to the conference room, I turned my phone off. Dana may not still be spying, but I wasn't taking that chance.

When we reached the conference room, everyone was indeed waiting. Angelica was at the head of the table, James to her left and Beren to her right. But that was it. The other agents had left.

My cheeks heated at James's, Beren's, and Angelica's knowing smirks. Why was I even embarrassed? It's not as if we'd actually done anything remotely R-rated. Sheesh.

We quickly sat.

Angelica nodded. "Good, now that we're all here, we can start. I won't keep you long. It's been a trying few weeks, and I'm afraid the PIB's been turned upside down. It will take a few days for us to get everything back in order, but I don't foresee too many problems. I've spoken to one of our directors. He's sent me documentation appointing me as Agent Pembleton's replacement." She paused, and we all took a moment to think of him and reflect on this afternoon's tragedy.

Then she continued. "James will be my replacement. Congratulations, Agent Bianchi." Angelica smiled and shook his hand. I grinned. It wasn't every day I got to see my awesome brother promoted.

"Thank you, Agent DuPree." He gave her a nod.

"Now, on a more serious note." She waved her hand in an arc: her silent cue that she'd created a bubble of silence. "What I'm about to tell you comes under our top-secret investigations. None of this is to ever be spoken about to anyone but each other, Millicent, or Olivia. They will also be brought into this secret task force."

Were we going to investigate where Dana went? That would seem like a job for the PIB, not something secret.

"Lily, those photos you took at the warehouse contained an unknown man."

"Yes. Do you know who he is?"

"No, but he had a distinctive snake tattoo on his neck, which we've matched with a similar, smaller tattoo that was on both of the men you killed in the last few weeks."

Way to make me feel guilty. "It was in self-defence." I folded my arms and wriggled lower in my chair.

"We know that, Lily. I'm not criticising you. But this is a valuable piece of information."

Oh, crap, it totally was. I was such an idiot sometimes. *Focus, Lily.* "Sorry, Ma'am. You're right."

"Do you know what that tattoo means?"

Everyone shook their heads.

She held her gaze on me. "I can only assume it's some kind of group that Dana may have been working for. Your kidnappers also worked for the same group."

No. Freaking. Way. Where she was going with this, I did not want to follow. Dana had been out to get me the whole time? But how did she even know I'd ever show up? She'd been working at the PIB for years. Had she been planted to lie in wait just in case daughter followed mother into the witch-criminal catching business?

Will and James traded "oh, crap" looks.

"I see the penny has dropped for all of you. Good. She didn't come back for a promotion—she came back for Lily. Although why she didn't kidnap her, I don't know. We'll work on finding that out as we go. Also, there's one more piece of information I have. The tattoo was a snake with the word 'regula' before it and 'issam' after it."

"Do you know what it means?" I asked, because everyone else was busy thinking it through, probably trying to figure it out, but I didn't have the brainpower left. I needed this handed to me on a silver platter. I deserved that much after the day I'd had.

Angelica looked at me when she spoke. "The snake isn't just any snake; it's a python. Paired with issam, it forms the Latin word *pythonissam*. Regula is Latin for 'rule'. So, essentially the tattoo is stating Rule of the Witch. We have a lot of research to undertake, but I think we've found who's after you, and who took your parents." It was as if someone had punched me in the gut. I stopped breathing for a few beats. Her gaze shifted to James. His face was carefully neutral, but he blinked a few times. He'd been here for years trying to find any clue as to what happened to our parents. This would have shocked him too.

James turned my way. We stared at each other, and I knew neither of us would give up until we discovered the truth. This also meant I had a chance finding who was trying to kidnap me and stopping them. But how big was this group, and how powerful were they?

"If they supplied Dana with that ring, it would indicate they're well connected, or at least have lots of money and knowledge, wouldn't it?"

Angelica raised her chin in a half nod. "Yes, Lily, but until we know more, let's not assume the worst. So far, they've failed every time they've tried to take you. Now we have a real chance to find and neutralise them, and they don't know about any of the information we have on them. As far as they're concerned, we're no closer to catching them than we were yesterday or a month ago."

Well, that was something. I shut my eyes, needing some space from everything. Today had been another crazy roller-coaster of witchdom. I needed to get off the ride for a while.

"It's okay, Lily. I think we all feel a bit that way. Why don't we reconvene lunchtime tomorrow at my place?"

I opened my eyes. "That would be great, thanks. Oh, and can you get my phone looked at? Dana was tracking me with it." I slid it across the table.

James grabbed it. "I'll drop it into Tim on my way out tonight."

"Thanks."

"Good afternoon, team. I'll see you tomorrow."

She stood, and we all did the same. James and Angelica started a conversation and left together. Beren gave me a quick hug and winked as he left. He was too cheeky for his own good, but I'd get my own back one day if he ever asked Olivia out.

"So, I can't call you later." Will smiled.

"Ha ha, no, but even if I had my phone, I wouldn't be answering any calls. I think I'm going to sleep for a week."

"You can't do that. You'll miss our Saturday-morning run."

"Hmm, sleep or a first date with you?" I tapped my chin, pretending to think.

He grinned and grabbed me in a hug. "Once you've had one date with me, you'll want more. I promise."

"Mr Confident, aren't you."

"They don't call me Mr Tight Buns for nothing."

I laughed, remembering that night in the car when we'd been teasing Will about nude modelling for my art class. "I suppose they don't." I squeezed his bum cheek. What the hell was wrong with me? My hand had a mind of its own.

"That was rather cheeky, Lily."

"Oops, sorry. You said tight buns, and I had to check. My bad."

"Seriously, though, I'll make it up to you." There was no hint of joking in his voice, and I believed him. He pulled me closer and kissed the top of my head. I lifted my face and kissed his cheek, lingering for a moment longer than normal before pulling back and stepping out of his arms. If I didn't leave now, I didn't think I could trust myself to not grab him and kiss the hell out of him, and I was pretty sure neither of us was ready for that yet.

"I'll see you Saturday, Will." I was about to make my door when he spoke.

"Oh, and, Lily?"

"Yes?"

"You're not the only one who's waited a long time for this." He flashed his dimples one last time, stepped through his door, and disappeared.

As I made my door and travelled to Angelica's reception room, I couldn't get the stupid smile off my face. If anyone had told me today was going to end with my heart bursting with happiness, I never would have believed them. Not that life was perfect with a crazy witch and her equally nutty but powerful society after me, but at least we had somewhere to start.

I unlocked the door and made my way into the house, my grin still in place. "Hey, Liv," I called out.

"Lily!" she yelled from upstairs.

I started walking the two flights to her room. "Guess what?"

She met me at the first-floor landing. "What?"

I was surprised my idiotic grin hadn't given things away. "I think Will really likes me. We're going to start dating."

She jumped up and down, then hugged me. Today I'd filled my yearly quota of cuddles. "I told you he liked you. That's the best news ever."

"Wanna go downstairs and make some pancakes?" It was too early for dinner, but I needed food, some laughs with my best friend, and then sleep.

"You read my mind."

We linked arms and walked down the stairs. All my friends loved me again, the violence would stop because we'd caught the perpetrator—well, one of them—and things were temporarily right with my world.

Maybe being a witch was going to be okay after all. I guessed I'd find out soon enough, but at least I'd have backup this time.

We made it to the kitchen, which was thankfully devoid of the witch cage. I turned the coffee machine on and took out the ingredients for pancakes. As I got to work, I looked at Olivia. "Aren't you going to boil the kettle for a cup of tea?"

She shook her head. "I'm going to steer clear of tea for a while. I'm thinking a mocha coffee would be a good alternative."

"Coffee and chocolate. You can't go wrong." I grinned and got another cup out of the cupboard. Olivia grabbed a pan and put it on the stove. As we cooked, I thought about everything that had transpired that day.

The possibility of finding out what had happened to my parents terrified me, but at the same time, I was desperate to know. And if we found who was involved, we could finally bring them to justice. That was something worth working towards. James and I had ten years of justice to dispense. Suddenly, torture didn't seem as evil as I'd thought.

Olivia ladled pancake batter into the pan. "Lily, why are you smiling?"

"Oh, nothing. Just thinking about the future." And what I could do to those bastards who took my parents.

"I have a feeling it's going to be awesome from here on in. We're going to be working together, you're dating Will, and the baby's coming. So much cool stuff is happening." She grinned.

She was right: so much cool stuff was happening. I shrugged off thoughts of revenge and gave her a genuine smile, one borne from happiness. "I have a feeling you're right, Liv. And what better way to begin the rest of our awesome lives than eating pancakes together?"

We clinked coffee mugs in cheers, and Liv said, "Here's

to the future. May it bring us everything we've ever wished for."

That was something I could totally drink to. And we weren't asking for much, right?

Yeah, right.

ABOUT THE AUTHOR

USA Today bestselling author, Dionne Lister is a Sydneysider with a degree in creative writing, two Siamese cats, and is a member of the Science Fiction and Fantasy Writers of America. Daydreaming has always been her passion, so writing was a natural progression from staring out the window in primary school, and being an author was a dream she held since childhood.

Unfortunately, writing was only a hobby while Dionne worked as a property valuer in Sydney, until her mid-thirties when she returned to study and completed her creative writing degree. Since then, she has indulged her passion for writing while raising two children with her husband. Her books have attracted praise from Apple iBooks and have reached #1 on Amazon and iBooks charts worldwide, frequently occupying top 100 lists in fantasy. She's excited to add cozy mystery to the list of genres she writes. Magic and danger are always a heady combination.

ACKNOWLEDGMENTS

To my much-loved editors, Becky and Chryse. Thank you both for helping Lily shine. And a special shoutout to my cover designer, Robert Baird. This could be my favourite cover of the whole series. I just love how you take my ideas and make them come to life in the most perfect way.

And thank you to all the readers who are joining me on Lily's journey. To know you're enjoying the series brings me a crazy amount of joy.

ALSO BY DIONNE LISTER

Paranormal Investigation Bureau

Witchnapped in Westerham #1

Witch Swindled in Westerham #2

Witch Undercover in Westerham #3

Witch Silenced in Westerham #5

The Circle of Talia

(YA Epic Fantasy)

Shadows of the Realm

A Time of Darkness

Realm of Blood and Fire

The Rose of Nerine

(Epic Fantasy)

Tempering the Rose

Printed in Great Britain
by Amazon